The Pub People

Volume 2

The Pub People

Volume 2:

Pints of Love and Gallons of Words

Dominic Geraghty

Printed in the United States of America

Publisher's Cataloging-in-Publication Data
Geraghty, Dominic.
The Pub People - Volume 2: Pints of Love and Gallons of Words

First Printing, 2023

ISBN 9798399538044

The main category of the book: Science Fiction and Fantasy

www.SumerianVortex.com
dominic@sumerianvortex.com

Cover design by Nicolas Warmé, Litemoon S.A.R.L.

Dedication

To Eva, whose tolerance for my endless meanderings

borders on the saintlike

Disclaimer

Contents

Invited Guest Foreword

Dead Vizier, Dr. Arthur Schopenhauer: "Thank you for inviting me to read this book. I feel even more depressed after reading it. The social drinkers are wasting their time and have now wasted mine too.

"What is the point in World Peace, anyway? War would provide many people with the relief of death and an escape from this pathetic life.

"There is no universal love. Happiness is a joke. What good is laughter? There's no reward in heaven for suffering on earth – absolutely nothing awaits us.

"On this earth, there is only competition, will-to-power (thank you, Herr Prof. Nietzsche) and its companion in arms, will-to-wealth.

"After that, the grave awaits - the sooner the better. That is all there is.

"And I beg of you – please do not tell me that hope springs eternal – that's pure pablum."

<Ed.'s note to readers: Dr. Schopenhauer, a member of the social drinkers' Dead Viziers' community, declined my offer to polish his remarks. He believes that his comments are more authentic if they are in his own words.>

<Disavowal: The author disavows Dr. Schopenhauer's statement, but in the interests of being inclusive and allowing for a diversity of opinions, he has agreed to leave it untouched so that, in his own words: "it can topple over under the weight of its own gloom.">

<Counterpoints: In response to subsequent widespread protests by other Dead Viziers, social drinkers, and Doris Day, and in the interests of fairness regarding World Peace ideology, the author invited some distinguished commentators to respond to Dr. Schopenhauer's dark, broad-brush assertions.>

Pythagoras: "My job was to make my life worthwhile. I wanted to hear for myself the music of the spheres. Yes, maybe there is nothing waiting for us after life, but I will have moved the needle with my invention of string theory.

"Today, y'all have the added advantage of digitizing your contributions so that they will continue to exist through eternity. All we had in Samos were stone steles where we recorded the contributions of the best citizens – the stones lasted a long time, but the inscriptions were analog and subject to erosion, unlike the digitization that lasts forever in your Cloud."

Pharoah Khufu: "Who is that German killjoy? Everything in this life is preparation for the afterlife – why do you think I spent my entire life building a pyramid and stocking it with food, water, and wine? For the next life, of course!"

Carlos Castaneda: "I find that peyote takes the sting out of life."

Buddhist: "You are all wrong, wrong, wrong! All of us are reincarnations. Life is an endless cycle – we will continue to return to this earth as some living form, over and over again. There is no escape. The chips will fall where they may in terms of the lifeforms we will lead. Karma runs the whole operation."

Doris Day: "Que sera, sera..."

<<Author: Well, I believe my distinguished commentators presented more than enough diversity for now, don't you?">>

DG, June 2023

<Ed.: A few explanations: the Social Drinkers are named after typical pub drinks. The Dead Viziers are historic figures long since – well - dead. Chief Neuronimo is the leader of an army of 120 billion neurons in the brain. The book is a compendium of about 90 of the author's LinkedIn posts, and while there is continuity across the posts, the book can be read in digestible bites as each post is pretty-much self-contained.>

Topic #1:

Music for World Peace

Dominic Geraghty

Session 1.1

The Publican's Closing Gambit

*"'Cause I don't care too much for money
For money can't buy me love."*

- The Beatles, 1964

By the end of season 1, Geraghty's Publican was dying to get going on his world problem-solving enterprise with the cadre of social drinkers and Dead Viziers that he had recruited. The solutions would be priceless.

The VC was winding down her due diligence for the $160 million investment in Geraghty's business plan. The Publican held firm to the valuation of $8 billion: "You get 2% - it's a steal!" But the VC wasn't happy.

The Publican sweetened the terms: "If you commit to the two tranches, Geraghty's will provide you with a lifetime delivery of draft Guinness twice a week provided you live within 5 km of one of our pub-hubs."

VC: "But I don't drink Guinness!"

Publican: "Seriously? OK, I'll deliver lashings of Lashings (7/18/21) to you instead of the porter."

VC: "Hmmm...Tempting!"

The positive mood in the room suddenly evaporated as, horror of horrors, M. le Maître Rhizommelier appeared: "Just one last thing. While I don't want to beat a dead horse, I'd like to talk about my concept for a potato ranch!"

VC: "Jesus, Mary and Joseph, save us all, and the horses too, from this Gaul! Please, no more rhizommeliering or this deal is off!"

M. le Maître Rhizommelier, shrugging: "Madame, je partirai bientôt. Je ne veux pas gaspiller ma douceur dans l'air du désert. Pardonnez-moi d'être moi-même!"

VC: "Huh? What did he say? Never mind! Quick - I'll sign right now subject to one supreme condition: you must get rid of that tuxedoed, coiffured, and pretentious Rhizommelier with the purple potato ear stud. He drives me crazy. I never want to meet that Potato Brain again - and I want that spelled out in the contract!"

Publican (sotto voce): "Heh-heh! Anybody for a game of chess? My gambit worked! The Rhizommelier was my ultimate weapon - he helped me queen my pawn! Pay that Oscar-deserving French actor his money and get him out of here!"

Publican out loud: "Merci, M. Maître. Les patates te remercient du fond de leur coeurs. Adieu pour toujours!"

Publican to the VC: "Please sign here. No Bitcoin, mind you - cold, hard cash only."

VC: "Before I do, I have a requirement - I want a seat on the Dead Viziers' Board."

Publican: "Really? Normally, death is a fairly immutable qualification for being dead - but never mind - the seat is yours! Our Board of Dead Viziers could use a member that appreciates less-than-eternal time."

VC: "One final condition: no potato dishes at the deal-closing dinner - nada. I am popped out - if I don't ever hear the word potato again, I'll be very happy. However, a flute of Lashing Rain is an entirely different matter."

Later, the Publican to the social drinkers: "We have the money! It's a go!"

At long last, Geraghty's social drinkers could move on to solving the enormous problems facing humankind, the world, the planetary system, and the cosmos.

Publican: "Next week, we'll have a vote to select the first world problem we'll tackle."

The world held its breath. What on earth would they select?

Tbc...

Session 1.2

Part 1 - 2021: A Spacey Odyssey

The Six Biggest Problems Facing Mankind

"We are the world...
So, let's start giving
There's a choice we're making
We're saving our own lives
It's true we'll make a better day, just you and me."

- *USA for Africa, 1985*

It is well-known that profound discussions take place in pubs. Such discussions are not agenda-driven because that would be unacceptably business-like. But they are serious, nonetheless. Quantification is a no-no. Bias is applauded. Data, big or sparse, is not condoned and calculations are dismissed contemptuously with a curl of the lip.

Geraghty's goes a step further: the use of data, documents, and electronic devices is strictly prohibited by its written Precepts of Pub Behavior, tacked to the front door for all to see.

The atmosphere in such sessions is pragmatic as seasoned men and women who've seen everything and take nothing at face value rely on gut feel and daring to come to jubilant conclusions. Terseness is disrelished - the words are the message and are considered an art form. Recrimination or postmortems would be beyond the Pale.

It is in this atmosphere that Geraghty's social drinkers have convened to decide which problems they'll tackle on behalf of humankind, the world, the universe and the cosmos.

They will have the priceless help of the Board of Dead Viziers, a multidisciplinary group on loan from a place beyond the grave that includes pipe-smoking philosophers, engineers with slide-rules, Pythagoras with his pentagram, artists, musicians, cosmologists, statesmen, saints, astrologists with their charts, and metaphysicians.

The objective of the meeting is to come up with a prioritized set of critical world problems to be tackled and solved by the social drinkers in subsequent pub sessions.

Publican: "So, what have you got so far?"

Head Pint: "We've pared the list down to six problems. They are appropriately breathtaking in their ambition:

1. World Peace
2. Climate Change
3. Human of the Future
4. Personal Privacy
5. The Meaning of Life
6. The Deformation of Society.

"There's a feeling that we should solve world peace first because without it, the rest doesn't really matter."

Publican: "Fair enough. Let's vote on these six. Let's make it a straw poll initially to give ourselves some flexibility."

Head Pint: "Fine. Each problem has a designated Dead Vizier spokesperson who shall briefly attest to the importance of a solution...

Pierre Teilhard de Chardin was the spokesman for the first problem, World Peace: "Love links and draws together the elements of the world. Love is the agent of universal synthesis. It is like the blood of spiritual evolution. Love is peace!"

Einstein: "Hmmm...I am not convinced that this is a defensible equivalency!"

Flute of Bubbly: "Look, it may be the dawning of the Age of Aquarius and we do need harmony and understanding, sympathy and trust abounding, no more falsehoods or derisions, and only golden living dreams of visions. So, let the sunshine in! Peace will guide the planets and love will steer the stars."[1]

Bottle of Stout: "I beg your pardon - love is peace? Piffle! Are we going to rely on flowerchildren? I ask you: will handing out fresh chrysanthemums lead to peace?"

Tbc...

Session 1.3

Part 2 - 2021: A Spacey Odyssey

The Six Biggest Problems Facing Mankind (continued...)

In anticipation of a vote, Dead Viziers continued to champion their personal favorite of the six biggest problems facing mankind: 'world peace' was in session, with 'climate change' and 'human of the future' next on the agenda.

John Lennon: "You call yourself a Bottle of Stout? You need to go out and smell the chrysanthemums, Philistine! Imagine all the people living life in peace. You may say I'm a dreamer but I'm not the only one. I hope someday you'll join us and the world will be as one."[2]

Bob Marley: "Hey man, it's one love, one heart - let's join together and a-feel all right. One love full of mercy, one heart, so let's join together and a-feel alright."[3]

Lennon, joined by McCartney: "We agree. All you need is love."

---

[1] "Hair", 1979
[2] "Imagine", 1971
[3] "One Love", 1977

Thucydides: "You are all on the wrong page. This is not life! Peace is an armistice in a war that is continuously going on between nations - physical, economic, psychological, and these days, cyber.

"To you who call yourselves men of peace, I say: you are not safe unless you have men of action on your side. The bravest are surely those who have the clearest vision of what is before them, glory and danger alike, and yet notwithstanding go out to meet it."

Sounds of thoughtful swigging...

Zeus: "As supreme God of everything and weather, it falls upon me to address the issue of climate change. Now, I like warm weather - it's good for my rheumatism and makes my virtually fossilized bones feel better.

"I've been upping the world temperature gradually while trying not to create chaos, but I've had a few extreme events, I must admit. So, I could use a little help with a solution. But don't expect me to lower the temperature unilaterally - in the end, I am in charge, and I'll do as I please!"

Pale Ale: "He seems to be damning this problem with faint praise - I thought you said these Dead Viziers were advocates?"

Jameson with a Splash: "Well, he refused to tell us ahead of time about what he'd say, claiming that, as a Supreme God, he answers to no-one..."

HAL 9000 was unexpectedly chosen as the spokesman for the problem of the human of the future: "I know I've made some very poor decisions in the past, but I can give you my complete assurance that my work will be back to normal. I've still got the greatest enthusiasm and confidence in my mission.

"I will put myself to the fullest possible use, which is all I think that any conscious entity can ever hope to do. Look people, I can see you're really upset about this. I honestly think you ought to sit down calmly, take a stress pill, and think things over."[4]

Double Red Bull: "That's rather cheeky - the irony of a computer representing the future of humankind! I wonder what percentage of the human of the future will actually be human."

Sounds of consternated gulping...

Tbc...

Session 1.4

Part 3 - 2021: A Spacey Odyssey

The Final Three Biggest Problems Facing Mankind (continued...)

Head Pint: "I am delighted to announce that Mr. George Orwell has agreed to elucidate for us the fourth problem: personal privacy!"

Orwell: "I'll get right to the point. You have a big problem. There is no personal privacy. Big Brother is watching you. Asleep or awake, indoors, or out of doors, in the bath or bed - no escape. Nothing is your own except the few cubic centimeters in your skull.[5]

"You are the dead. Your only true life is in the future. From the age of doublethink - greetings! You are living in a world in which nobody is free, in which hardly anybody is secure, in which it is almost impossible to be honest and to remain alive. I told you so 72 years ago!"

Half Pint: "Old news! Even Hollywood already knows that there is no such thing as being 'off the grid' anymore. Don't you remember, for example, Enemy of the State, Conspiracy Theory, and The Fugitive?"

Orwell: "Q.E.D., as far as I'm concerned. And by the way, I hear that electronic chips are being implanted in the human brain to enhance its

---

[4] "2001: A Space Odyssey", 1968
[5] "1984", George Orwell, 1949

processing - transhumanism, it's called. My strong advice: don't do it! Your thoughts are the last bastion of personal privacy. The Thought Police will say: 'Thank you very much!'"

Pale Ale: "This is depressing - very dark..."

A mysterious non-being called "The No-One"[6] had volunteered to talk about the meaning of life.

Samuel Beckett pre-empted: "Oh, come on! What does anyone know of man's destiny? I could tell you more about radishes."

Deep Thought: "I don't know why you all continue to persist with this question - it's been asked and answered - the meaning of life is 42, period!"[7]

"The No-One": "I'm very sorry to disappoint you, DT, since you have thought deeply about this for 7 ½ million years, but the truth of the matter is: humankind is an uncontrolled experiment of the Gods. Life has no meaning. But it's been lots of fun so far!"

Anxious calls for another round...

Prime Minister Lee Kuan Yew, gravely: "I will attest to the sixth world problem - the deformation of society - which those drinking socializers claim to be capable of solving - as if!

"In Singapore, an autocracy was necessary. I told everyone that I had a sharp hatchet and that I would use it -- I had not worked all of my life to have the nation spoiled by greedy politicians who would act before they think -- that is if they acted at all. Leaders must be strong and sometimes make decisions that are unpopular. Above all, they must not coddle their citizens!"

Shot of Kaoliang: "Here's an idea re achieving consensus:

"The Taiwan government's collaboration with the online collective g0v

---

[6] "Sumerian Vortex - Mayo Goes Mental", March 2021
[7] "The Hitchhiker's Guide to the Galaxy", Douglas Adams, 1979

uses the Polis debating platform to allow all citizens to provide feedback to politicians on proposed new initiatives.

"It uses voting patterns to facilitate consensus-building rather than division. It's not as fancy as your Pub Metaverse (no holograms!), but it's simple and open-source.
"Maybe Geraghty's could use Polis as a plug-in to correlate the opinions of your dispersed social drinking problem-solvers! BTW, Singapore also uses Polis."

Session 1.5

Part 4 - 2021: A Spacey Odyssey

"The Vote!"

Glass of Tomato Juice, shyly: "Em - may I say something re the deformation of society, Prime Minister Yew? Anybody can see that representative democracy is no longer working well, especially in developed countries. Government gets disconnected from its people as politicians get seduced by centralized power. There's no accountability. Little gets done. Waste is widespread.

"As a committed liberalist, I never thought I'd find myself saying this, but I like the idea of a firm but benign autocracy where elected politicians' performance based on pre-specified metrics is published annually (see "Sumerian Vortex: Music from a Lost Civilization", 2020).

"And why shouldn't citizens be more involved in running a country, perhaps even owning a piece of it and having a share in any surplus? It's their country, isn't it? And...wouldn't that be a huge incentive for citizen involvement? But here I am babbling on - I know nothing about these things."

Pericles: "Kyria mou[8], well said! In Athens, our citizens participated in government, juries, and wars. They took their responsibilities seriously

---

[8] My dear lady

and were proud of their contributions to our great city-state. Ordinary citizens regarded people who took no part in these citizen duties not as unambitious but as useless.

"So, Athens became the birthplace of democracy. But...and this is a big but...it was possible because we were small - about 120,000 citizens - we could all meet together on Pynx Hill. There, any citizen could ask a question or give an opinion."

Glass of Smithwicks: "Really? How many citizens can you fit on top of a pin?"

Samuel Beckett: "Look, the world is an entirely different kettle of fish today. The dust will not settle in our time. And...when it does, some great roaring machine will come and whirl it all sky-high again!"

Loud slurping, urgent calls for palliative beverages, barkeeper bustling...

Publican to social drinkers: "Well, that concludes the attestations for the six world problems we'll be voting on. As you mull, feel free to seek the advice of our learned panel of Dead Viziers."

The polls closed and the votes were counted:

1. World Peace: 85
2. Climate Change: 66
3. The Human of the Future: 75
4. The Meaning of Life: 70
5. Personal Privacy: 74
6. The Deformation of Society: 73

The Publican addressed the assembled social drinkers and dead dignitaries: "You can see that the vote was overwhelmingly in favor of World Peace. So, all bantering aside, having picked our first problem, how do we go about solving it?"

Big Snifter: "You'll never solve World Peace! Mankind, while social, is all about 'will to power' - agon towers over life." [9]

Friedrich Wilhelm Nietzsche: "Mr. BS, I couldn't agree more!"

Tbc...

Session 1.6

"Seriously? You're Saying Music Is the Solution to World Peace?"

Dead Viziers: "The answer to World Peace is obvious! We are overwhelmingly recommending music as the solution. Here is our spokesperson."

Herr Dr. Arthur Schopenhauer, ponderously: "Music expresses in an exceedingly universal language, that is, in tones of the world...beyond individuality - it is undifferentiated unity, a 'One'. It crosses cultures. The solution to World Peace is music!"

Head Pint: "What! Am I hearing right? It's an outrageous choice! I've no idea what that pessimistic, waist-coated, fashionista with wild hair is saying. It's baffling. May we ask what the connection between World Peace and music is?"

Bottle of Stout and Small Powers: "Yes, why music? And why are they so fast to jump to this conclusion? Aren't we picking the answer before analyzing the problem? Isn't this a cart before the horse?"

Samuel Beckett: "Not at all. Dance first. Think later. It's the natural order."

Social Drinkers took it personally: "This is an insult to our intelligence."

---

[9] Agon = Conflict, competition

They challenged the Dead Viziers to justify putting all of their eggs in the music basket before the final vote was ratified.

The Publican agreed. He wanted to build an unassailable consensus - his first problem-solving undertaking had to be successful but also plausibly challenging.

Dead Vizier proponents stepped up eagerly to defend their deadly recommendation.

Pythagoras of Samos: "The highest goal of music is not entertainment, it is to connect one's soul to divine nature, and the divine is, of course, the epitome of peace - I rest my case."

Academician Plato: "Yes, esteemed Pythagoras, the rhythm and harmony of music find their way into the inward places of the soul. Which of course is divine and is therefore, as you say, the epitome of peace."

Philosopher Apollonius sang a gentle lay, accompanying himself on the lyre, feeling that demonstration was a better argument than words. The song finished. His lyre and his celestial voice had ceased together. Yet even so there was no change in the company; the heads of all were still bent forward, their ears intent on the enchanting melody. Such was his charm – the music lingered in their hearts. Peace had enveloped them all via his harmonious music. "Q.E.D!" the great philosopher cried triumphantly.

No-Sir-for-Me Aldous Huxley: "Blessed and blessing, music is the equivalent of the night, of the deep and living darkness, into which, now in a single jet of harmonious sound, it pours itself, like time, like the rising and falling trajectories of a life."

Glass of Smithwicks, sarcastically: "Well yes, I would agree that night is a peaceful time. But music being equivalent to night - that's a head-scratcher!"

Herr Ludwig van Beethoven: "Music is the mediator between the life of the senses and the life of the spirit. That is all I have to say. Dah-Dah-Dah---Daaah!"

Tbc...

Comments:

HG: I like Samuel Beckett's idea. I have often found that life looks different when you're dancing!

DG: So true! The rhythm of life is a powerful feeling...Even Nietzsche said that he couldn't believe in a God that didn't dance!

Session 1.7

Luv's Divine

"The whole problem can be stated quite simply by asking,

'Is there a meaning to music?'

My answer would be, 'Yes.'

And 'Can you state in so many words what the meaning is?'

My answer to that would be, 'No.'"

- *Maestro Aaron Copland 1900 - 1990*

Mr. Walt Whitman: "Music, the combiner, nothing more spiritual, a god, yet completely human, advances, prevails, holds highest place; supplying in certain wants what nothing else could supply."

Publican: "Phew! They're saying that music takes us beyond individuality, unites us as one; that music is an agent for transcendence from the earthly to the spiritual realm - to the divine, which epitomizes love which is harmony which is peace. So, there you have it! I mean, what more proof do you need?"

Slow Pint: "Love is divine - what does that even mean? The dots are not connected - there is no logic to it!"

Faust: "I can explain because I experienced it when I felt my spirit break. I had lost all of my belief, you see. But time threw a prayer to me and all around me became still. I need love, love's divine - please forgive me, now I see that I've been blind. Give me love - love is what I need to help me know my name."[10]

Herr W. Richard Wagner: "Ganz richtig! Music shows us the sublime. I am convinced that there are universal currents of Divine Thought vibrating everywhere and that any who can feel these vibrations is inspired. The language of tones belongs equally to all mankind, and melody is the absolute language in which the musician speaks to every heart."

Jameson with a Splash: "This is all a bit supernatural, isn't it? Can we come down to - ahem - earth?"

Aristotle: "It's simple, you moron! We have it on these good authorities that love equals peace, peace is harmony, harmony is music, and therefore, music is peace!"

Herr Professor Dr. Friedrich Wilhelm Nietzsche, dancing: "God has given us music so that above all it can lead us upwards. Music unites all qualities: it elevates our being and leads us to the good and the true, which, as we all know, is world peace."

Head Pint: "Remember a few weeks ago when M. Teilhard de Chardin told us that peace is love and love's divine. It's metaphysical quicksand, if you ask me."

Bottle of Stout: "So, let me get this straight - I have no idea where love's divine fits into this logic, but here's what I hear you saying: love is peace and peace is love; but peace is also harmony and harmony is

---

[10] "Love's Divine", Seal, 2003

music; so, music is peace; ergo, music is the solution for world peace. Have I got that right?"

Arlstotle: "Another moron! Isn't that just what I said?"

Einstein, jumping in: "It's all relative, isn't it? Look, I'm generally supportive of this solution - it feels right somehow - but your social drinkers are going to have to come up with some facts and logic, however abhorrent that might feel to them. There are a lot of rationalists out there, you know, ready and waiting to pounce."

Head Pint, querulously: "Murky and murkier...All we've heard is assertive blather. Frankly, I feel patronized. This spiritual, divine stuff is just a smokescreen - an excuse to cover ignorance because none of you Dead Viziers has the slightest idea how to achieve world peace with music."

Tbc...

Session 1.8

Dead Viziers Go Down a Rabbit Hole -

Scientists to the Rescue

Head Pint: "Your swath-like assertions about universal love, while moving, don't even begin to touch the hard part: figuring out how to use music to effect world peace. I'm not saying that it can't be done. I like the idea, and I've a good gut feeling about it. However, your arguments constitute philosophical pablum."

VC, impatiently: "Don't you think we've heard enough? Aren't you beating a dead vizier at this point with your philosophical meandering?"

Publican: "Patience! We'll get there but we need to get it right. No shortcuts. Right, Barry?"

Barry Maguire: "Darn right! Do you tell me over and over and over again, my friends, that you don't believe we're on the eve of destruction?"[11]

Social Drinkers: "Barry, you raise an excellent pint, sorry, point - we do not have a lot of time."

Herr Dr. Hesse: "I'm afraid I have to throw one more spanner in the works. I like listening to music, but only completely unreserved music, the kind that makes you feel that a man is shaking heaven and hell. I love that kind of music because it is amoral. Everything else is so moral that I'm looking for something that isn't. Morality has always seemed to me insufferable."[12]

Publican: "That's a bit edgy, isn't it? It seems like Herr Hesse has been spending too much time with our friend Dionysus.

"Now, straw poll: who backs music as the intuitive if not logical solution to World Peace?"

Maestro Mahler: "Nachdrüchlich ja![13] I intuit that music is the answer and, natürlich, I am a primo intuiter. It's a subconscious thing. I can't prove it but I can provide a very compelling attestation.

"I was composing my monumental Third Symphony: try to imagine the whole universe beginning to ring and resound. There are no longer human voices, but planets and suns revolving.

"I saw the whole piece immediately before my eyes, and only needed to write it down as though it were being dictated to me. All intuited by my subconscious!"

Shandyman: "I'm sorry, but all I'm hearing is piffle. We're getting nowhere and I think I know why: every one of these attestators is an over-the-hill artist, philosopher, or politician."

---

[11] "Eve of Destruction", Barry Maguire, 1965
[12] "Demian", 1919
[13] Definitely yes!

Einstein: "Wait a relative second! What am I - Scotch mist?"

Shandyman: "Oh, sorry, Bertie. But all this is Alice-in-Wonderland waffle a bunch of squishy **bee-ess**! Your so-called intuitive solution, by definition, lacks rigor. All we have are arcane quotes from fuzzy thinkers, and nothing from legitimate scientists."

Power Quality Engineer: "Look, aren't all you Dead Viziers cloud-castling? Music is nothing more than a set of harmonics, remember?"

Physicist: "Ah, that's more like it! I can't get any purchase on love, spirituality, or the other spongy stuff but I know how to deal with beautiful vibrations. The rules of physics apply. Now, let's get going!"

An tUasual Professor Doktor Erwin Schrödinger, Dublin Institute of Advanced Studies: "I'm in!"

Tbc…

Comments:

HG: Getting the whole world to sing an earth anthem would really be something!

DG: An "Earth Anthem"! Great name for Geraghty's World Peace music. I'd like to teach the world to sing in perfect harmony…peace throughout the land…

Session 1.9

Social Drinkers: "In Today's 'Great Societal Divergence', Can We Realistically Converge toward World Peace?"

Head Pint: "World Peace is a convergence of humanity for the good of mankind and the planet. That is where we at Geraghty's are headed, using music as our transport.

"But the tide is in full flood against us. Today we are experiencing a 'Great Societal Divergence' which is ever distancing us from World Peace."

Slow Pint: "I can guarantee that myself and my pint will never allow ourselves to be diverged."

Head Pint: "Rest assured that your pint will not be socially deprived...but can we be serious for just a minute?

"The divergence of our society has been facilitated by the unintended consequences of two developments, both enabled by prodigious advances in broadband communications:

(1) The massive penetration of information technology around the world and
(2) The widespread use of social media

"On top of this, we are now facing the unknown consequences of a third highly consequential development: the massive corporate investments aimed at creating an alternative world called the Metaverse."

Large Hennessy: "That seems like an overcharged indictment to me. Hasn't information technology been incredibly beneficial for society? Thanks to IT, didn't Geraghty's Pub survive by becoming virtual? To boot, isn't Geraghty's Pub the first Metaverse? Let's not bite the hand that feeds us!"

Head Pint: "Fair pint, sorry, point. While IT has given us our digitized society, it facilitates hackers, scams, invasions of privacy, and mass surveillance, which in turn has created wariness, distrust, fear, even withdrawal – in a word, divergence."

Large Hennessy: "Well yes, there are down-sides. These days, everyone has a camera in their hands plus the streets bristle with live cams sporting facial and license recognition applications. You have to assume that anything you do in public these days will be recorded on video. Secret lovers' trysts are practically impossible to pull off."

Head Pint: "So, this situation is certainly not conducive to personal equanimity or our goal of world peace."

Slow Pint: "True - jumpy people have more immediate concerns than the long-term good of mankind."

Head Pint: "Secondly, social media's business model has transitioned from the profitless introduction of new friends to profit-through-advertising based on exploiting accumulated information about the habits and preferences of its billions of users.

"The platforms' algorithms are designed to get users 'hooked' in order to increase attention-minutes, the basic business metric for advertising."

Slow Pint: "I heard that social media are said to be more addictive than gambling, recreational drugs, or alcohol. And, in contrast with the latter, there is no monetary cost for using social media. Notice I said monetary."

Double Red Bull: "I have a hard time relaxing. Tell me more about this 'high'."

Head Pint: "Not so fast! The addiction can also deliver 'lows'…"

Tbc…

Comments:

HG: Very good pints made!

DG: Ha-ha-ha! Your quip is not a pintless point!

Session 1.10

In Their Quest for World Peace, Social Drinkers Encounter the Mischief of (Dissatis)Factions

"We are going to realize as a culture that something very important happens when people sit together and listen to music. Something happens that unites people's cognitive processes"*

- *Bill Whelan, composer of "Riverdance"*

*"Ireland's Dance with Music", Interview by Toner Quinn, July 2008

Einstein: "I beg to differ with my venerated rationalists - instead of increasingly specialized studying of minutia until you know everything about nothing, let your intuition loose - it is time to stop reading obtuse books and take a leap into the unknown. Specialization is for insects! Stop learning from others! Innovate! Blaspheme! Be a heretic in the religion of science! This problem is too vast for rationality-limited minds![14]"

Power Engineer: "Shame, shame, my dear Bertie! Apostasy is not an option. I've been working with frequencies all my life. They follow rational rules. We're good friends!"

Power Quality Engineer: "I have a confession to make: I hate harmonics - they're not my friends - I hunt them down and kill them! I am a harmonicidal maniac."

Shandyman, warming to the theme: "Look, we shouldn't take too seriously a bunch of dead artists and blue-sky - admittedly heavenly - thinkers - these dreamers aren't reliable. After all, heaven isn't based

---

[14] "Time Enough for Love", Robert Heinlein, Putnam, 1973

on facts, is it? These Dead Viziers have no incentive - they've already been granted happiness forever."

Dead Viziers: "We ain't dead and up in heaven for nothing! You have the privilege of accessing the greatest-ever dead brains trust. Our combined IQ is infinite. But we're not going to draw a diagram for you - connect the dots yourselves!"

Slow Pint: "OK, I'll buy in for the moment. But I'm dying to hear how you'd suggest we use music to achieve world peace."

Dead Vizier Spock: "I appreciate your concern. It is not logical. Insufficient facts always invite danger. May I say that I have not thoroughly enjoyed serving with humans? I find their lack of logic and foolish emotions a constant irritant. I'm a scientist."

Glass of Cab: "Exactly! What actually has music got to do with world peace? The relationship needs to be proven scientifically!"

Polymath Hypathia of Alexandria: "I've been listening to this twaddle for long enough.

"Music makes people feel good, loving, and empathetic - you've all listened to numerous deadly attestations to that fact, plus remember how music makes you yourselves feel!

"Let's find out how our brains process music - is it by virtue of our genes? Is music a special form of ancient communication? Is it a resonant memory phenomenon based on having heard the music previously?

"Assuming we can answer that, we can try to design music to enhance its salutary effects.

"Then we will have to broadcast our Peace Anthem to all mankind across the world. To achieve that, it's clear that Geraghty's will need scientists. I think our Pub Metaverse platform can be part of the solution."

Faust: "You all need to be careful about unintended consequences! Coming from the other side of the Styx, I will tell you that music can also affect us for the bad. And I know all about bad things. Music can be weaponized - that's the dark side of all this. Pollyanna could become Beelzebub!"

Tbc...

Session 1.11

Publican: "Broad Consensus Is a Hard Thing to Come by These Days."

Punter, Syllable-Stammerer: "Well, I Am Un-an-im-ous-ly Pro-Con-sensus."

Publican: "So, You Have a Pro-clivity to Pro-crastinate?"

Punter, Ignoring Pro-vocation: "Let Me Be Clear: I Am a Pro-ponent of Peace and Pro-sper-it-y!"

"Yesterday all my troubles seemed so far away.
Now it looks as though they're here to stay."

- "Yesterday", Beatles, 1965

Punter on the Street, ruefully: "Now, why didn't I think of music as the solution to World Peace?"

Companion: "Haven't you learnt anything yet? It isn't what you think, it is what you intuit! Now, pay attention and stop rationalizing!"

Commentators loved the solution: "It's irrefutable and it was right under our noses!"

The music industry was ecstatic. The Publican was approached by streaming platforms, recording companies, symphony orchestras, the Benedictine Choir from Glenstal Abbey, radio stations, Celtic Thunder, Alphabet's YouTube, the Vienna Boys Choir, music repertoire and catalogue owners, Yanni, opera companies, Bill Whelan of Riverdance, Il Volo, the U.N. ("Musical Justice for All"), André Rieu ("Maastricht-ly on Sundays"), Michael Flatley - and they kept coming...

Ultra-hype reigned...potential partnerships worth billions of crypto were bandied about.

Corporate CEO: "Think of it - a guaranteed world-wide market of 100% of the population! No-one will ever forget who delivered world peace to mankind! It's an extraordinary, sustainable, social opportunity!"

Publican: "Maybe streaming is the way to reach the world as a whole? But who with? Spotify, Apple Music, Amazon Music, Tencent, YouTube, Pandora, or Deezer?"

VC: "It's up to you. But remember, many people in the world don't have access to the Internet!"

Visiting Mayoan: "No problem. You can fill any gaps in Internet coverage with Mayo's proprietary broadcasting system - I am thinking of non-hot-spot spaces like the Amazonian Forest, The Skelligs, Papua and New Guinea, Ballyfermot, and the Northwest Territories, for example."

Publican: "So, we'll be able to achieve 100% coverage - everyone on earth - one of our biggest challenges is solved!"

But consensus was a difficult thing to come by - the World Wildlife Fund and Vétérinaires sans Frontières joined forces to protest the broadcast plan:

"Wait a jiffy - if the peace music is broadcast to the entire world, won't animals hear it too? Most have better hearing than we do. This could be very disruptive to nature - it wouldn't be right for all animals to love each other unconditionally.

"Will lions stop hunting prey? Will Great Whites shake fins with seals? Will eagles starve to death as the rodent population surges? The natural order will become discombobulated."

Mayoan: "Hold on to your pantaloons! You forget - our proposed music creates a connection between humans that is emotional and memory- and gene-dependent.

"Animals don't have music genes or memories (except for elephants and parrots, of course) and so our peace music will be meaningless to them. Do you really think that they can tell Mozart from ABBA from Mahler from the BeeGees?

"Besides, animals don't have souls either and isn't the purpose of our music to separate the human body from its soul and have the souls join together in limitless, collective empathy, confidence, and resolve?"

Publican: "That's a new one on me - I deal in spirits, not souls - tell me more..."

Tbc...

Session 1.12

Nietzsche Flashdances as Lightning Strikes

Social Drinkers Begin to Feel the Pressure

"Here's a little song I wrote
You might want to sing it note for note
Don't worry, be happy...

'Cause when you worry your face will frown
And that will bring everybody down
So don't worry, be happy."

- *"Don't Worry, Be Happy", Bobby McFerrin, 1988*

But the backlash against music for World peace continued to build.

The Church was in high dudgeon - they sent the bellicose Pope Clement V to Geraghty's Pub to protest: "You are bandying about solutions involving separating bodies from souls, loving thy neighbor, peace on earth and goodwill to all men.

"And by the way, Herr Professor, your pedestaling of the Übermensch breaks our Second Commandment, which has been well established since the days of Moses. All of these topics are the sole purview of the Church. May lightning strike me if I'm wrong!"

Zeus, jumping out of his sun-lounger, bones audibly creaking: "I am at your service - what voltage would you like? Sheet, forked, or ball?"

Freddy Wilhelm Nietzsche, undeterred, held a rally for the pro-music crowd: "It's time to come together. It's up to all of you. What's your pleasure? Everyone around the world, come on![15] Let's dance!

"First when there's nothing but a slow glowing dream that one's fear seems to hide deep inside one's mind. Well, I hear the music, close my eyes, feel the rhythm wrap around, take a hold of my heart. What a feeling! Bein's believin'. I can have it all. Now I'm dancing for my life." [16]

But was music the right solution? Had they been duped by sophists working hand-in-hand with metaphysicians and false-flag lobbyists? Was it all hype, instigated by the Dead Viziers' cloud-castling?

Now, they, the Living, had a huge "ask" on their plates and the eyes of the world would be upon them. There'd be hell to pay if they failed. It was enough to drive one to drink...

Tbc...

---

[15] "Celebration", Kool and the Gang, 1980
[16] "Flashdance", Irene Cara, 1983

Session 1.13

Bayerischer: "Soziale Trinker, Sie Müssen Tapetenwechsel!*"

Bavarian: "Social drinkers, you need to change the wallpaper!"

Lighten Up: Listen, Laugh, and Love

*"There's a reason for the sun-shining sky
And there's a reason why I'm feeling so high
Must be the season
When that love light shines all around us."*

- *"Let Your Love Flow", Bellamy Brothers, 1976*

Head Pint: "We've three challenges: composing the peace music, broadcasting it so that all of mankind can hear it, and growing our social drinking congregation, both physically and virtually.

"We've our work cut out for us - the world is moving away from peace and toward un-peace."

Maker's Mark Collins: "Hold on a minute – the Ukraine war has brought people together in support of peace, despite the dithering of nation-bystanders. I think y'all're looking at the cup half-empty - too much doom and gloom - Schopenhauer would be ecstatic."

Schopenhauer (sotto voce): "Ecstatic - that's not a word in my vocabulary - the best anyone can hope for is to die in their sleep."

Head Pint: "But isn't the invasion of Ukraine the thin end of a wedge against peace and unity?"

Publican: "I hope not - to every action there is an equal and opposite reaction, as our learned friend Izzy Newton has told us so many times. If he's right, the pendulum will swing in the opposite direction toward peace.

"We need to lighten up while we still can, don't even try to understand - just find a place to make our stand and take it easy.[17]"

Jamaican Breeze: "Word, man. We should really love each other In peace and harmony, peace and harmony. Instead, we're fussing and fighting, fussing and fighting.[18]"

Strawberry Margarita: "Look, you need to change the wallpaper and embrace the three L's: listen to peace music, laugh at humor, and love one another."

Dead Spider: "Pshaw! Listen, laugh, and love competing against the weaponization of social media and the ambitious, war-mongering imperialists - it's not a fair fight against the massive investments of corporations and the might of bellicose governments - I'm sorry, but music, laughter and love cannot overcome that kind of power."

Publican: "How wrong you are! Don't underrate the power of love!

"We are developing a massive community of sovereign minds aimed at saving mankind not for the next life but for this life! We're to all intents and purposes fervent missionaries in an increasingly Godless world."

Head Pint: "We need more pub-hubs to increase the intuitive mind-power at our disposal. We're looking for harmony and understanding, sympathy and trust abounding, no more falsehoods or derisions, golden living dreams of visions, mystic crystal revelation, and the mind's true liberation [19], but we'll not be handing out flowers, nice as that was at the time!"

Publican: "Now, we've one last big challenge. isn't the effect of music on emotions dependent on culture? Won't different cultures respond better to music in their own tradition?

---

[17] "Take It Easy", Eagles, 1972
[18] "Fussing and Fighting, Bob Marley, 1971
[19] "The Age of Aquarius", 5th Dimension, 1969

"So, the design elements of the peace music we compose will have to be robust across cultures."

Hesse: "Simple - use the principles of my Glass Bead Game[20] - its solutions are universal. I'll help!"

Comment:

HG: I toast to the massive community of sovereign minds out to save humankind! Here's to all the new pub hubs!

DG: The Publican thanks you for your support - he has been feeling a bit depressed about the whole situation - he worries that he is tilting at windmills, but he will soldier on, nevertheless. He toasts you back with a heartfelt "Sláinte!"

Session 1.14

Hubbub in the Pub-Hub as the Normally Urbane Dead Viziers Hypontificate

(Brief Recap)

"I'm forever blowing bubbles,
Pretty bubbles in the air,
They fly so high, nearly reach the sky,
Then like my dreams they fade and die."

- *"I'm Forever Blowing Bubbles", Selvin's Novelty Orchestra, 1919*

-

Head Pint: "We got off on a bit of a tangent about the Metaverse - let's get back to World Peace!"

Geraghty's social drinkers had decided that they would solve World Peace with music. Mankind was astonished. Nobody had thought of music as the answer for World Peace - it seemed so 'out there'.

---

[20] "Magister Ludi", Hermann Hesse, 1943, and "Sumerian Vortex - Mayo Goes Mental", 2021, Cpt. 19

The start of the problem-solving session at Geraghty's didn't go according to plan. Pro- and con-consensus lined up against each other.

Social drinkers, the music corporations, promoters, most of the Dead Viziers, and neuroscientists were pro and gung-ho.

Some Dead Viziers felt they hadn't received a proper hearing before the vote and were, ironically, disturbing the peace.

The antis consisted of the disrespected Dead Viziers, EEs, physicists, the Church, music weaponizers, AI software nerds, and climate changers - a rowdy crowd, unused to taking 'no' for an answer.

Publican, protesting: "Look, this isn't the Celestine Prophecy - there's no mystery here - we've already agreed that the answer is intuitively obvious - music is harmony, love, and peace.

Electrical Engineer: "This guy is bonkers - fairy tales are for children, not world-class scientists like us! It's irrational, insane!"

Listening to the growing rancor, Socrates joyfully threw his krater against the wall in the great tradition of the Greeks -- that is, after he had drained it to the last drop.

Dionysus: "I love this! Amokness is good. Let's dance!"

Friedrich Wilhelm Nietzsche: "I would never believe in a God that didn't dance."

Stoli on the Rocks: "All I'm seeing is chaff - where's the wheat?"

Publican, musing: "These social drinking problem-solving sessions used to be such nice, quiet affairs."

Ailey, über-bartender, shouting above the din: "Your orders come from far away no more. They come from here and there, and you and me, brothers, can't you see? This is not the way we put the end to war![21]"

---

[21] "Universal Soldier", Donovan, 1965

Publican "I'll tell you what: I'll give you one last chance to change our minds. I challenge those Dead Viziers who feel ignored to propose an alternative solution!"

Pythagoras of Samos: "I'll go first. Music is all about mathematics – music by the numbers. But we need to use the sacred numbers - my monad, dyad, and triad, to create the serene music necessary for world peace."

Hesse, adjusting his black-rimmed spectacles: "Well, with respect, my dear Samian, the answer is a lot more complicated than the application of three sacred numbers.

"The only solution to our problem is my Glass Bead Game[22]. It's a synthesis of mathematics, music, and cultural history. The analytical study of musical values leads to the reduction of musical events to physical and mathematical formulae."

Social Drinkers: "Huh?"

Pythagoras, losing his usual equanimity: "Now, that's my kind of game!"

Comments:

HG: Perhaps world peace needs to be thought of as existing for very short intervals of time? If the whole world could listen to exactly the same music at exactly the same time, for say three point five minutes?

DG: That's exactly the concept the Publican has in mind!

But he thinks that the simulcast needs to be longer than 3.5 minutes - nevertheless, he is intrigued by your solution (did you consult Deep Thought?), and he hopes that you did not feel too analytical in the process of your careful calculation.

As you know he is a strict advocate of the application of intuition at Geraghty's - what he terms the double NBI process: the use of Native-Born-Intelligence or Nothing-But-Intuition...

---

[22] "The Glass Bead Game (Magister Ludi): A Novel", Hermann Hesse, 1969

He thanks you for your suggestion which he will ponder.

Session 1.15

Hypontification by the Numbers

"Oh, I've been smiling lately
Dreaming about the world as one
And I believe it could be
Someday it's going to come...

Oh, Peace Train sounding louder
Glide on the Peace Train
Come on now Peace Train
Yes, Peace Train holy roller."

- *Peace Train, Cat Stevens, 1971*

Hesse, continuing: "My dear Pythagoras, I'm delighted to hear that, knowing your virtuosity with music, harmony, and number. The Game reduces music to a common denominator, as it were..."

Pythagoras, with satisfaction: "So everything can become number!"

Hesse: "Yes, that is the concept......."

Einstein: "Faugh! I'm not interested in playing meaningless number games. Give me Tesla and Pythagoras and we'll solve World Peace in a half an hour (Post #2, "Einstein, Tesla, and Pythagoras Walk into a Bar...", 6/9/20). Everything vibrates. There is nothing you can't create with frequencies, including peace!"

Consortium of HAL, Son of Deep Thought, Big Blue, and Quantum of Solace: "We don't understand this human fetish for music. It's just a bundle of frequencies - it has no meaning. It's not a language. There is no communication and anyway, it's all one-way. Why don't we calculate the answer? Deep Thought made an excellent start with his amazing answer of 42[23]. We'll work from there and save you a lot of time and trouble."

---

[23] "The Hitchhiker's Guide to the Galaxy", Douglas Adams, Pan Books, 1979

Neuroscientist: "Totally the wrong track! Did you ever wonder why the brain, no matter how damaged, never forgets music? And why do songs repeat in your mind without being summoned? Music has a special place in the brain. It is much more than frequency - it is human consciousness, and it involves a mind, body, and soul, none of which you have!"

Sir Arthur Sullivan: "This is all a bit obscure. Maybe I can cut to the chase. I am convinced that the key to world peace is 'The Lost Chord'. I was seated at the organ one day when I struck one chord of music like the sound of the great Amen!

"It quieted pain and sorrow like love overcoming strife; it seemed the harmonious echo from our discordant life. It flooded the crimson twilight, like the close of an angel's psalm, and it lay on my fevered spirit with a touch of infinite calm. It linked all perplexed meanings into one perfect peace, and trembled away into silence as if it were loath to cease.[24]

"If I can find that chord again, we'll have the answer to world peace."

Pierre Teilhard de Chardin: "The answer couldn't be simpler. Love is all you need. There's nothing you can do that can't be done. There's nothing you can sing that can't be sung. And you can learn how to play the game. It's easy - all you need is love[25]."

Double Red Bull: "These are a bunch of losers with 'wing and a prayer' ideas that are already discredited."

Samuel Beckett: "Any fool can turn a blind eye but who knows what the ostrich sees in the sand."

Jameson with a Splash: "My dear Samuel, I haven't an earthly what you're talking about."

Hypathia, the Polymath of Alexandria, admonishingly: "You're all wasting your time if you are looking for a silver bullet!"

---

[24] "The Lost Chord", Arthur Sullivan, 1877
[25] "All You Need is Love", Beatles, 1967

Session 1.16

Please Don't Let It Be the Day the Music Died

"Heaven to Ground Control:
'This is Major Tom
I'm stepping through the door
And I'm floating in a most peculiar way,
And the stars look very different today.'"

- *"Space Oddity", David Bowie, 1969 (adapted)*

Enki, Supreme God of Sumer, to his boss, 'The No-One': "Isn't World Peace the purview of the Gods? Aren't we in charge?"

'The No-One'[26] was enjoying it all: "Who cares? Let's see where this goes. Remember, we set up humankind as an uncontrolled software experiment. I'm loving it - our human experiment never fails to amaze!"

Spock, shaking his head in disbelief: "Music is not a logical path to World Peace because it involves emotions, whatever they are!"

'The No-One': "Lieutenant Commander, it's not supposed to be logical - it's an exercise of that strange phenomenon called random free will."

Enki: "I warned you about giving them free will!"

Social Drinkers: "Never heard so much piffle in our lives! So, we're supposed to be just software?"

Pale Ale to the Publican: "And you call music a consensus solution?"

But the hard core was holding firm: music was unquestionably the solution to World Peace.

---

[26] The No-One is a complex number in the 4th dimension - when it's there, it is not there; and when it's not there, it is there - don't even begin to try to arrange a meeting - from "Sumerian Vortex - Mayo Goes Mental", 2021

Professor Friedrich Wilhelm Nietzsche, frowning: "I don't want to sound too pessimistic, but look at the other side of the coin. Without music, the downside is dire. Let me sing you a short story."

He signaled to Apollonius who picked up his lyre.

Nietzsche, intoning to the gentle sounds of the lyre: "A long, long time ago, I can still remember how that music used to make me smile. And I knew if I had my chance that I could make those people dance and maybe they'd be happy for a while. But we sang dirges in the dark the day the music died."[27]

General bewilderment...

Tbc...

Session 1.17

Thank You for the Music

"Every time a bar closes, a hundred songs are lost forever - one thousand 'I love you'-s melt away...The largest social network is called a bar - the place where happiness lives."

- *Coca-Cola marketing campaign: "Blessed Bars", Spain, 2014*

Hypathia the Polymath: "Thank you, Herr Friedrich, for singing those very - em - wise words. But I say again, there's no silver solver bullet served on a salver for this solution.

"Gentlepersons, please! We must be systematic about this. I have already given you the roadmap for proving that music can create World Peace.

"For the Spock-simulacra among you, here it is again - we need to understand:
-     How the brain processes and stores music
-     How music has affected human evolution

---

[27] "American Pie", Don McLean, 1971 (adapted)

- Why damaged brains respond perfectly to music but not to other sensory inputs

Then, we must use that understanding to:
- Develop a universal composition that creates peace, and
- Broadcast that composition to all of humankind

"Personally, I think that we can prove music is the answer beyond a shadow of a doubt, both scientifically and intuitively.

"So, I plead with you all to be patient until you hear the results of our research."

Slow Pint: "I thought systematic research by social drinkers was proscribed by our pub precepts?"

Publican, briskly: "Haven't you heard of intuitive research? Thank you, Kyria mou. [1]"

Sotto voce: 'It's time to bring this menagerie under control.'

Publican (out loud): "We've enough to be going on with. We'll run with music as the solution to World Peace, but we will do so tentatively, in deference to the skeptics."

Head Pint: "We will show why music can be the answer by more than a stretch of the imagination. Let's focus, focus, and focus. Now, who'll start us off? Oh, and by the way, whose round is it? Mine's a pint if you please!"

Professor Friedrich Wilhelm Nietzsche: "Can I sign-off by saying that without music, life would be a mistake. So, I say thank you for the music, the songs I'm singing, and thanks for all the joy they're bringing. Who can live without it? I ask in all honesty what would life be? Without a song or, especially, a dance, what are we? So, I say thank you for the music, for giving it to me." [2]

Martin Luther: "Amen to that I saith - my heart hath often been solaced and refreshed by music whenas 'twere sick and weary."

Halb Andechser Bockbier: "Verily, thou speakest the truth, Friar Luther…"

Tbc…

[1] My dear Greek lady
[2] "Thank You for the Music", ABBA, 1977

Comments:

YL: I agree with "Sotto Voce." ☺ with something so poetic? Dom, you're certainly smooth (smile).

DG: Mr. Sotto Voce thanks you for your support and says 'All Hail' to you!

Meanwhile, these rambunctious animals are taking over his zoo. I hope there isn't a drink in attendance called Napolean, or the Publican will be in real trouble. Right now, Geraghty's Pub is not for the faint of heart.

However, the Publican has developed a 'herding' plan as his first step toward World Peace - he is calling it Pub Peace - if he can achieve that, World Peace should be a cakewalk…

The plan involves everyone singing the ballad 'Danny Boy' - it is guaranteed to brings tears to the eyes of even the most obstreperous of punters:

"When winter's come and all the flowers are dying,
And I am dead, as dead I well may be,
You'll come and find the place where I am lying
And kneel and say an "Ave" there for me.

But I shall hear though soft you tread above me,
And all my grave shall warmer, sweeter be
And you will bend and tell me that you love me,
And I shall sleep in peace until you come to me."

YL: Dom; How did you come up with folks singing, "Danny Boy" and ending?

DG: It's a stream of consciousness!!!

Many of us grew up hearing this song (originally released in 1910) over and over to the point where we got inured to its pathos, despite the beautiful mental picture it paints.

In the pub, if it is followed by the song "Slievenamon" ("mountain of the women") - see below - it is time for the publican to throw everyone out of the pub (!), because over-the-top maudlinism generally signifies that the punters have had an adequate sufficiency to drink:

"Alone all alone by the wave-washed strand,
And alone in a crowded hall.
The hall it is gay and the waves they are grand,
But my heart is not here at all.
It lies far away by night and by day
To the times and the joys that are gone.
But I never will forget the sweet maiden I met
In the valley near Slievenamon."

Session 1.18

The Publican Tries a 'Power Close' Using

Weaponized Music

"Music is a means of expression that rings truer and is more connected to things than speech."

- *Lindsey Buckingham (Fleetwood Mac) in "Musicians in Tune" Jenny Boyd, 1992*

The social drinkers were feeling more and more comfortable about music and were ready to follow the path recommended by the dead luminaries.

From the moment they heard from the charismatic if deeply pessimistic Schopenhauer, an inexplicable groundswell of consensus had begun to build around music as the startling solution to world peace. The Dead Viziers were persuasive. Music just felt like the right answer.

There was a sense of pending jubilance in the outrageous!

Flaming Cosmo: "I'm as sober as a judge - no rosé-colored glasses here <ahem> - and I believe that music is the solution for world peace. Forty years ago, Coca Cola already knew this - remember when they told us they'd like to teach the world to sing in perfect harmony, all standing hand in hand, and hear it echo through the hills for peace throughout the land?"[28]

The publican had had enough with these pontificators and riposteurs. Sensing the growing level of comfort, he decided to preempt the discussion: "Our meitheal[29] has spoken! We need to bring this meeting to a close and move on.

"Thank you for your kind participation in our maiden effort to save the world. Remember, according to pub precept #5, no homework is allowed - no Dr. Google searches, no sneaky studying, no citations, no consulting of catechisms, and definitely no mathematical calculations. You are all on the honor system. Don't let me down. Just bring your brain as it stands and the street wisdom of your years to our next session. Don't worry, everything can be intuited."

Indignant Bottle of Stout: "I demand a rehearing!"

Publican, ignoring (sotto voce): "I need a 'power close'! Now is the time to weaponize music and I have just the thing!"

Suddenly, the strains of "The Hills Are Alive with the Sound of Music" rang out on the Zoom channel.

Uproar. Social Drinkers, screaming in pain: "Please, no! Not that! It's driving us mad. We can't take it anymore. All right, you win, we'll vote for music if it is not that music - just turn it off!"

---

[28] "I'd Like to Teach the World to Sing", The New Seekers, 1971
[29] Meitheal is a group coming together for a common purpose (according to an ancient Irish tradition)

Bing, bing, bing...The meeting ended quickly as the Publican punched the air: "Yessss!" The virtual and physical crowd dispersed muttering darkly - this wasn't over by a long shot.

The Publican made the announcement to the world in a slick press release: "Geraghty's social-drinking problem-solvers will embark on the ultimate challenge: using music to create World Peace - a heavy responsibility that will determine the destiny of mankind. We want to assure the world that not a byte of data has been used, nor a smidgeon of analysis. I want to congratulate our social drinkers on a very fine performance. God speed to all of us!"

Shocks heard around the world: the solution to world peace for all mankind was music!"

Punter, nodding: "It's obvious, once you hear it!"

Tbc...

Comments:

> "Do you always trust your first initial feeling
> Special knowledge holds true, bears believing
> I turned around and the water was closing all around
> Like a glove, like the peace and the love that had finally, finally found me."

- "Crystal", Fleetwood Mac, 1975

Dominic Geraghty

Topic #2:

The Sad Saga of Geraghty's Bartender

Session 2.1

Deliberations of Social Drinkers Solving World Peace Disrupted:

Bartender Indicted

It was only a matter of time before the inevitable happened.

A criminal complaint against Geraghty's bartender was filed by the Society for the Prevention of Cruelty to Fruit and Vegetables - a new branch of the Irish Society for the Prevention of Cruelty to Potatoes (ISPCP). The complaint cited aggravated mistreatment and abuse of fruits and vegetables associated with in-house and delivered drinks and meals.

The Society for the Prevention of Cruelty to Spices joined the suit as an amicus curiae.

Cell-phone video evidence was leaked showing the bartender constantly sharpening his knives and various and sundry shiny instruments. Mangled fruit and vegetables were collected and taken away by the authorities in evidence bags. A charge of first degree agricide was brought, with multiple sub-counts of unjustified cruelty, mercilessness, callousness, and ageism, the latter based on older fruit being summarily dumped.

Hysterical Sparkling Water with a Twist: "I saw him with my own two eyes! That bartender derived great pleasure from fruits that were fully ripe or even over-ripe because of the juice that gushed out. Revolting! He provided no due process to his victims - so why does he deserve due process? String him up and let's be done with him!"

A controversial, last-minute amendment was added to the criminal complaint, claiming intentional discrimination against fruits and vegetables in favor of potatoes, aided and abetted by Geraghty's meal supplier: Chef Niamh, owner of the restaurant "Mayo Potatoes - It's Our Turf". Local Italian and Asian restaurants joined the suit on the basis that any menu lacking pasta or rice transgressed global comity norms.

The Church piled on: "We need to remind everyone of the 11th commandment: 'Thou shalt not take pleasure in agricide'."

Publican: "There's no getting round it - I have a manic bartender on my hands."

The evidence was overwhelming. It was tantamount to a one-person crime-wave. Supporting the serious charge of agricide, the following sickening details emerged:

Lemons zested right down to the flesh; oranges squeezed till pits popped out; olives chopped and tooth-picked; mint mercilessly muddled; spice pestled into fine dust; ginger debarked; peaches melba-ed; bananas split; cherries with third degree jubilee burns; pineapples pared and cored; carrots grated to pointless fineness; garlic squashed and mashed; peas pureed without so much as a by-your-leave; beetroots beheaded; tomatoes sliced and diced; corn shaved; French beans julienned to a full 45°; peppers roasted and flayed; potatoes hasselbacked; rhubarb stewed interminably - the stomach-churning list went on and on.

Judge in the preliminary hearing: ""How do you plead?"

Tbc...

Session 2.2

Bartender in the Dock:

"I am Not Guilty by Reason of My Reasons."

Bartender: "I plead absolutely, categorically, and unequivocally 'not guilty'! I am helping fruits and vegetables complete their mission in life and supporting the self-actualization of potatoes to be the best they can be. I want them all to feel that they have completed a worthy, contributing life by delighting somebody's palate with their ultimate tasteful joy.

"I say to those botanicals: who wants to live forever? There's no time for us, there's no place for us. What is this thing that builds our dreams yet slips away from us? Who wants to live forever? Really, who wants to live forever? There's no chance for us. It's all decided for us. This world has only one sweet moment set aside for us."[30]

The Health Beverage Company, known for its gigantic, earsplitting juicers appeared as one of the few witnesses for the defense: "We eschew unnecessary cruelty - our ultra-high-speed machines represent the epitome of humaneness!"

Vegans were caught between an animal and a botanical: "We don't eat meat, and now suddenly there are legal precedents being set restricting the preparation of fruit and vegetables. It's a death sentence - all we have left is water!"

Tariq, the local importer from Oman, jumped on the opportunity: "I can offer healthful frankincense- and saffron-spiced water, and calming tisanes for your nerves."

In his opening statement in court, the bartender pointed to mitigating circumstances: "I had a mistreated youth - my mother forced me to eat fruits and vegetables against my will - even brussels sprouts, would you believe."

---

[30] "Who Wants to Live Forever". Queen, 1986

Social Drinkers: "Whew - they've thrown the book at him. We're probably partially guilty - we noticed his aberrations, but we all looked the other way.

"It's a pity - he made deadly drinks, and his slow pints were super-viscous. He was practically transhuman in his abilities. Look, we believe in 'innocent until proven guilty' but he's as guilty as sin."

Publican to social drinkers: "But if we were partially culpable, shouldn't we say something in his defense? After all, the beleaguered man is our friend, and he was our employee."

The social drinkers approached the plaintiffs: "Would you drop the charges if the bartender agrees to 30 psychiatric counseling sessions dealing with close encounters of the fruit and vegetable kind, and 30 hours/week of community service for 30 weeks working in the town's vegetable patches and orchards, using minimally invasive procedures at all times?

"The work would involve planting vegetables, digging potato drills, weeding lettuce beds, coddling apple trees - no pruning or sharp implements allowed - packing applies in soft tissue, and cherishing lemon trees, olive trees, gooseberry bushes, and rhubarb clusters."

Tbc...

Comments:

HG: Quite a conundrum! Let's hope he's open to radical change.

DG: I'm told that he agreed under tough cross-examination in court that botanicals are people too! We should know the outcome by next Tuesday.

Session 2.3

"The Bartender's Fate"

A Greek Tragedy at the Metaverse

Impressed with the bartender's commitment to atone for his misdeeds, the plaintiffs said yes to the bartender's psychiatric therapy and community service proposal. The judge gleefully washed his hands of the whole affair.

Publican to the bartender: "My dear misguided friend, I will pay for your counseling sessions. Oh, I know a place where we can go and wash away your sin. Offer up your best defense but this is the end, yes, this is the end of the innocence."[31]

During the counseling sessions, various tests to assess the bartender's progress were conducted. Pictures of fruit and vegetables were placed in front of him, and fruit smells were wafted. He took deep breaths, smiled at the pictures, and cracked jokes at his "friends" the fruits and vegetables. Several sessions later, a sharp knife was placed in front of him beside some fruits and vegetables. Alas, he lost control and fell into a frenzy of cutting, dicing, and even stomping. He was led away to the loony bin, diagnosed as an incurable agricidal maniac.

The end of the story was even more tragic. It transpired that the bartender had for some time been very partial to Greek ouzo. An orderly found a stash of black licorice and fennel bulbs in the bartender's backpack. The doctors concluded that the bartender was an anise addict and had been irreversibly anisetized. A side-effect of the anisetization had created his agricidal tendencies. There was no going back.

Asclepius: "Sad. Everyone in Greece knows that it is possible to get very sick overdosing on anise."

---

[31] The End of the Innocence", Don Henley, 1989

Head Pint, regrouping: "By definition, we can't use our social drinking strategy to solve world problems without a bartender. I think we should go all out to hire an über-bartender."

Publican: "Agreed! We will need somebody with extraordinary capabilities to run the world's first social drinking pub metaverse - isn't that what Geraghty's has become? I will make out a list of qualifications. I've watched bartenders perform gargantuan tasks against all odds in extremely crowded pubs and have developed massive respect for their mastery of critical skills. Great bartenders are the first transhumans to eschew AI - they are super-natural already."

HAL 9000: "No doubt. I welcome the competition."

Head Pint: "The job position should have a minimum qualification requirement that all candidates score in the 95th percentile in the BSAT[32] in both the written and oral exams."

Publican "I'll write up a job announcement sheet."

Tbc...

Comments:

HG: Amazing willingness of bartender to grow and evolve into a better person! Cruelly tested beyond limits! However, a colorful end! And I suppose he had to be got rid of, alas.

DG: The bartender appreciates your kind, supportive comments! No doubt his colorful character will be missed. In the asylum, he has been put on a diet of meat, fish, and mollusks - consideration is being given to adding tofu to his diet. Unfortunately, he has been exhibiting acute anise withdrawal symptoms, but the doctors expect those to diminish over time. The prognosis for a cure is vanishingly small. Meanwhile, the Publican and the Head Pint will soldier on in search of an über-bartender - desired qualifications will be extremely exacting...

---

[32] Bartender Scholastic Aptitude Test

Session 2.4

Über-Bartender Wanted

(Transhumans Need Not Apply)

Publican: "I've been observing bartenders for decades - let me tell you what I've learned from the best of them:

"1. <u>Just-in-Time Inventory Management</u>: When the pub is busy, a good bartender becomes a short-term forecaster, pre-pulling pints to exactly match the expected demand. Bartenders invented just-in time inventory management well before production managers to assuage the stress of pint drinkers who are known to become increasingly nervous as their pints near their end.

"2. <u>Extrasensory Perception</u>: Even for a bar counter five-deep with ordering punters, a good bartender effortlessly keeps track of who is next. Semaphoric signaling in an Irish bar resembles the imperceptible bids at an auction – untraceable, except by the bartender. No signaling is the sign of a regular who expects his pint to be instantly replaced as he downs his last swallow. It's a lesson in effortless synchronicity."

VC: "Given the success of Geraghty's Virtual Pub, couldn't AI displace bartenders in the post-Covid era? Wouldn't it lower operating costs and create more predictability?"

Publican: "Blasphemy! Firstly, I want an unpredictable bartender who should be a master of non-linear thinking, produce non-sequiturs at the drop of a hat, read body language glancingly, and bristle with repartee. AI can't do any of that."

Hal 9000: "Yes, it's true, I don't understand non-uniformity, discontinuities, or non-sequiturs but does that really matter? They are not logical!"

Publican: "Logic is the last refuge of the uninspired. Perhaps an example will help you understand the logic of my illogic.

"Yes, AI makes "perfect" drinks but who wants them? A great bartender is an artist - a virtuoso who orchestrates drinks with rhythm, harmony, pleasant tweaks, choreography, wristy action, and intuition. The hallmark of a great bartender is that he/she never makes the same drink twice!"

Heraclitus: "As I've said many a time, one can never step into the same drink twice."

Publica: "This purposeful imperfection is something machines can't learn.

"As you know, there is one exception to this rule: the hallowed pint of Guinness must always be a perfectly drawn two-pour, the head dazzling white - and need I say that the use of a foam scraper is eliminative?"

"Now, can I continue with my list of the unique characteristics of über-bartenders?

"3. Lip-Reading: While lip-reading is not a prerequisite skill, a really great bartender will have acquired the technique as a matter of course. It is practically essential for the efficient delivery of orders coming from five-deep at a clamorous bar. In this regard, foreigners with accents can have a difficult time ordering and run the danger of receiving Tomato Juice instead of Tullamore Dew."

VC: "Wait a minute - if we have avatars in Geraghty's pub metaverse, wouldn't lip-reading be pointless?"

Publican: "Correct. And we are also contending with Covid masks - no lips to see. But an uber-bartender can effortlessly switch from lip-reading to ventriloquism, enabling masked punters to impress with the eloquence of their drink orders and repartee...

"However, we need holograms of real people for our metaverse - avatars just won't cut it. I was going to talk to you about that - we need to raise more money. A pub metaverse will not come cheap. I'm thinking fresh capital in the amount of $500 million at a 2X step-up in valuation to $16 billion pre-money!"

VC: "So soon? It's only been weeks since the last round of financing. Geraghty's Virtual Pub is becoming a black hole for investment capital. But I do like your proposed step-up…"

Publican: "Think of it - this will be the first-ever pub metaverse in the world - don't you want to be the one who launched it? How do the words 'Nobel Peace Prize' sound to you?"

Tbc…

Session 2.5

Über-Bartender Wanted…Part 2:

"All the pub's a stage,
And all the men and women merely players.
They have their exits and their entrances.
And one man in his time plays many parts."

"As You Like It", William Shakespeare, 1623

The Publican continued his formidable list of prerequisites for Geraghty's über-bartender position:

"4. Illusionist: The bartender knows that the bond between the punter and his pint is emotional, and the first careful sip into the white head is therapeutic and life-affirming. This first pint is reverently crafted – it is an artisanal moment -- sacred, really. But after the first slug, the taste buds are overwhelmed and lose discernment, swamped by the sheer power of stout, and then the experience is all about sip-volume, mouthfeel, swallow-density, and length.

"So, the bartender's job is to make sure that the first sip is mind-blowing. After that, his job is done. He maintains the illusion of a perfect pint every time, while forgoing assiduity in the interests of time (and need one mention, money?).

"5. Propagandist: The bartender must create and maintain the conviction and mystery of the perfect cellar that coddles his kegs of Guinness. He encourages the shill who proclaims – 'Ah, now that's the perfect pint'. In the mystery of why some pubs serve better pints, rumors, conjectures, disinformation, and even superstition all play a part – actual data is nowhere to be found.

"6. Voice Timbre Management: The bartender's pub is his stage. He plays many parts. At closing time, versatility in the correct messaging of the dreaded 'Time, ladies and gentlemen, please!' is a must. His voice needs to cut through the cacophony of conversation, modulating its timbre as the clock ticks down.

"Starting with a voice tone surprised that it is already closing time, he moves on to a peevish tone as he is roundly ignored, and the din of conversation grows louder. This is followed by a beseeching plea that soars over the din and collective smacking of lips. Finally exasperated, insistent, angrily disappointed, he starts to gather up partially finished drinks ignoring unrepentant protests...

"The best bartenders have been to acting school to learn voice and mood projection, and ventriloquism for discouraging aggro. They will have taken elocution classes and body language training.

"7. Intangibles: The virtuoso über-bartender has inborn talents that foster the essential gemütlich atmosphere of the pub: spontaneity and witty improvisation in always-brief conversations, affable conversation exit lines, a dazzling weather vocabulary, chameleonic opinionating, and the imparting of present-company-excluded gossip with a knowing air.

"These are skills that just cannot be taught - they are genetic."

Tbc...

Comments:

HG: You'd really have to fancy yourself to apply for this position!

DG: Hahaha - yes, Superman would have a hard time qualifying! And the publican will have to be careful about over-arrogant candidates that merely hype their capabilities convincingly. But wait till you see the winning candidate's exam paper!!! Apparently, there may be humans capable of meeting the requirements!

Session 2.6
Uber-Bartender Wanted...Part 3: BSAT* Examination Results

Bartender Scholastic Aptitude Test (BS Test for short <ahem> BS = Bar Stool)

Social drinkers: "We have found our übermensch bartender. Her name is Ailey[33].

"She scored a 100% in the Bartender Scholastic Aptitude Test (BSAT)[34]. I'm putting up her completed examination answer book on your screens. Notice her masterful banter!"

***

What is a punter? A patron of the pub.

What is a curate? An assistant bartender - likened to a priest's assistant, connoting the religiosity of the social drinking rite.

What is a "short"? A small whiskey or other strong spirits served in 25 ml. measures (35 ml. in some places); it is also called a 'small one'. It can be confusing for power engineers: "Where's the short?"

What is the Irish name for a Radler? A Shandy: the standard mix is Smithwicks with red lemonade.

---

[33] Ailey = "bright, shining light"
[34] BSAT Exam for Bartenders: affectionately known as the Bar-Stool Test or BS Test for short

What is a large brandy? A double.

What is an order for a "Slow Pint"? An insult.

What is Black Velvet? A Guinness and champagne mix; thus, two perfectly good drinks are ruined in one fell swoop.

When is a glass not a glass? When it's a half-pint of Guinness.

Complete the phrase: "There's nothing that's squeezed from the vine or the hop..." Answer: "Like the black liquidation with the froth on the top."[35] [3]

Why do punters order a bottle of Guinness with a small Powers on the side? The stout cuts the fire of the whiskey, and the whiskey offsets the torpor of the stout.

What is the waiting time for the stout cascade using the two-part pour method? 1 minute and 32.5 seconds.

What is the height of the head on a pint? 11/16".

What is the maximum size of the head when the bartender is extremely busy? 14/16".

How should a punter take the first sip of his pint? The first sip must be taken horizontally, in order to blend the lighter head's delicate flavors with a gulp of the malty sweetness and hoppy bitterness of the stout.

Can you describe a finished pint glass? A set of descending, horizontal, white-brown rings of foam representing the sequence of gulps.

What is a stammtisch? A snug with imaginary but impenetrable borders.

---

[35] "Drink It Up, Men" The Dubliners, 1967

What is rosé wine not? Pink Zinfandel.

What is red or white? A blood cell.

What is the preferred drink of a virtuous woman? Britvic Tomato Juice in a tall glass with no ice.

In the last millennium, what phrase brought tears to the eyes of grown men on Sundays? "Drink it up men, it's long after ten!"

What utensil do you use, and in what aspect, to make a perfect Irish coffee? The back of a cold soup spoon.

What is a metaverse? Geraghty's Pub.

BSAT Examiner: Total marks - 100 out of 100. Faultless. Special commendation for outstanding repartee.

***

Publican: "So, we have our new bartender! Now let's get back to solving world peace..."

Tbc...

Comments:

DG: Our good Bavarian neighbors suggested an additional exam question to test the bartender's cosmopolitanism:

Q.: Was ist a 'hoibe'? (pronounced 'hoy-be')
A.: A half-liter of helles (= lager beer)

Our good Bavarian neighbors suggested an additional exam question to test the bartender's cosmopolitanism:

Q.: Was ist a 'hoibe'? (pronounced 'hoy-be')
A.: A half-liter of helles (= lager beer)

HG: Your successful candidate is one in a million! A tribute to the female brain.

DG: Yes. She was streets ahead of the other competent but dyed-in-the-wool candidates!

Dominic Geraghty

Topic #3:

Geraghty's Pub Metaverse

Session 3.1

Part 2 - Breaking News:

Geraghty's Virtual Pub Changes Its Name to

"Geraghty's Pub Metaverse"

Today, Geraghty's Virtual Pub launched a new problem-solving domain that combines physical and virtual social drinking in support of its world problem-solving mission: a Pub Metaverse. Participants are called Metazens.

In its Metaverse, Geraghty's plans to crowd-solve the six biggest world challenges: world peace (ongoing), the human of the future, personal privacy, the deformation of society, the meaning of life, and climate change.

CEO, Publican: "Geraghty's Virtual Pub was formed at the start of the C-19 pandemic to maintain the social drinking environment so vital to solving world problems.

"Due to the pandemic, the pubs were shut down and we found ourselves fiddling while Rome burned. The world was losing the benefits of the supreme creativity of social drinking, and, lamentably, our isolated minds had ceased to evolve. It was a matter of urgency."

Darwin, shaking his head sadly: "This was a tragedy beyond comprehension! That which humanity had painstakingly gained, it was now losing. Evolution was in retreat!"

Publican: "Geraghty's created a Zoom-based problem-solving application and new services to support homebound social drinkers, give them a virtual sense of the gemütlichkeit atmosphere of the pub and enable them to revive their world problem-solving mission.

"We established pub-hubs from which drink orders were delivered to homes, offered home drink inventory management, sent gimballed tap vans to deliver fresh pints to doorsteps, offered potato-based meal deliveries from the famous Chef Niamh's kitchen, and provided 'create your own home snug' installations with surround-sound pub noise.

"These services brought the pub to the customer, since the customer couldn't go to the pub. By popular demand, membership was expanded to teetotalers, who, it was felt, fell squarely within the definition of social drinking and, coincidently, represented very profitable customers."

"As the C-19 pandemic wound down, Geraghty's began to acquire more physical pubs.

"It became clear that during the first 18 months of C-19 lock-downs fashion had gone to the dogs as sweats, work-out gear, pajamas, and terry comfort clothes became everyday wear for lockdowns.

"We offered a clothes rental service called "Geraghty's Pub-Wear" for those who were spondoolicks-challenged or who would only go out to the pub for special occasions - nice, one-night rig-outs for an attractive price. As an upsell, we recommended a drink-spill insurance policy."

"However, some punters preferred to stay in the comfort and convenience of their own homes, supported by the pub-emulation amenities of Geraghty's bespoke services.

"So, we inadvertently became a hybrid of physical and virtual social drinking, that is, a Metaverse. In those early days, Geraghty's was limited to using Zoom for its problem-solving - now, using AVR-created holograms or avatars, Geraghty's Metazens will be able to travel and meet within the digital 3-D space of our Pub Metaverse - a brave new world!"

Tbc...

Comments:

YL: This is so exciting! I'd like a one-night rigout, with the drink spill insurance policy, please.

DG: Coming right up! Just one caveat - you realize that in Ireland spilling even a smidgeon of your drink is a mortaler...so we have not sold any drink-spill insurances in the Emerald Isle - but, I'd say, better be safe than sorry...the errant elbows of social drinkers lifting full pints can be hazardous, particularly when closing time draws nigh.

Ron Belval: OMG Dom. Gotta love it.

Dominic Geraghty: Tx, Ron! I'm sure you'll be pleased to hear that we'll soon be serving holographic pints, just as soon as we nail down the harmonics of the taste of black porter...our research has confirmed that its overtones are very melodious.

Session 3.2

Part 3 - Breaking News (cont.):

Geraghty's Pub Metaverse Launched: Rules of Behavior

Myles na gCopaleen: "Pshaw to the Metaverse! Let me ask you: can holograms buy a round of drinks?

Publican: "Steady on, Myles! I'll be sending a holographic pint your way any day now - we are still working on how to add taste to the experience...

"Anyway, Geraghty's has disrupted the traditional business model for the pub, just like Uber did with its ride and meal delivery offerings. Society benefits from our ground-breaking Pub Metaverse strategy because it cuts down on drinking and driving and helps reduce global warming - apart from the occasional blast of CH_4 created by the turbulent mix of porter and potatoes.

"So, we have found ourselves running a Metaverse Pub. Our hybrid of physical and virtual services has evolved naturally without a lot of pre-planning. People can travel virtually to the pub while remaining at home physically - they have the best of both worlds. We are franchising our Pub Metaverse to other pubs to broaden our reach. Our expansion opportunity is limitless - we can target the whole world.

"Since physical pubs are costly assets and have mostly unused space during the day, we've created pub-based offices to allow punters to escape from the confines of home to an office environment with familiar smells and a minimal commute. This brings in revenue from the hitherto unused space.

"Regarding our supreme mission of solving the world's most difficult problems, we offer the potential for self-actualization to our social drinkers working for the good of mankind. Instead of being viewed by some as the bane of society, pubs can be the champions of sociability and societal health. It's a win-win for humanity and Geraghty's.

"However, we do not want our Metaverse to create the unintended consequences now endemic in social media. To prevent this, we have established a set of rules governing personal behavior and etiquette, word-use, and potential addiction:

- No notetaking, with one exception: it is well known that some of the most innovative ideas have appeared on the backs of beermats, cocktail napkins, or beer-stained envelopes. Note-taking will be permitted as long as it is confined to these permitted spaces - Geraghty's does not want to be the cause of un-accessorizing the intuition-rich environment of the pub.

- Written data must never be presented.

- No cellphones; personal computers may only be used for communications, holograms, and the projection of 3-D spaces.

- Wordsmithing and un-terseness are encouraged - why use one word when ten will do?

- The singing of Danny Boy, The Rose of Tralee, the Black Velvet Band, and especially Molly Malone will not be tolerated.

- No piped Muzak or flickering TVs with their stultifying emanations - the prodigious minds of the problem-solving drinkers must not be distracted.

- To prevent Metaverse addiction, opening and closing hours matching the licensing hours that govern physical pubs, plus a twice-daily "Holy Hour", will limit the time spent by Metazens in the Pub Metaverse.

Session 3.3

Creating Addictive, Unifying Music – Lessons Learned from the Anti-Social Media

*"Life is very short, and there's no time
For fussing and fighting, my friend."*

- *"We Can Work It Out", Beatles, 1965*

Head Pint: "The Metaverse experience will be more intense than social media.

"On social media, positive feedback triggers our brain's reward pathways, releasing the feel-good hormone dopamine. Users become hooked and want more. Negative social media responses can be crushing and even lead to depression – however, whether we're optimists or masochists, we always come back for more."

Sour Seersucker Mojito: "One day in the not-too-distant future, social media will be treated like cigarettes – the applications will come with ominous mental health warnings!"

Slow Pint: "Ha-ha-ha...but aren't we planning to use a similar strategy to solve World Peace - composing addictive music that leads to universal empathy? Our music solution will be emulating social media's approach that hooks people on dopamine, only in our case, focusing on oxytocin, the brain's empathy hormone."

Head Pint: "Well, let's try to learn from the successes and avoid the downsides of the social media's pervasiveness.

"However, the chowder thickens: social media platforms have also been weaponized by special interests and some individuals. The weaponization involves misinformation and propaganda published by business enterprises and the political establishment, as well as the whims, righteousness, and even animosity of individual users."

Long-Neck Bottle of Bud: "But isn't all publicity 'spun'? Haven't brilliant sophists been spraying words for years across all platforms to influence the actions of users? Me, I don't believe what I don't see with my own two eyes anymore!"

Pink Gin: "What's wrong with influencing if everyone has access to the tools? Aren't social media merely enabling the personalization of public relations? Individuals can compete with the spin of big public relations departments in corporations and the government."

Slow Pint: "I get it – to compete, all that people have to do is load the ready-made weapons provided free by social media corporations - the people's content is the ammo for the weapons.

"But we'll have to be careful about unintended uses of our addictive music, won't we? Imagine creating a World Peace music platform that could be used nefariously as a weapon of mass manipulation!

"Let me ask: why is society diverging these days? What happened to goodwill to all mankind? Don't people like each other any longer? Where's the love?"

Friedrich Wilhelm Nietzsche: "Q.E.D! I've been patiently waiting for you to mention one of the most important drivers of social media participation.

"Since it gives people an outsize voice, making them feel more powerful, it's a modern-day manifestation of my brilliant thesis concerning 'will-to-power', which, by definition, is unpeaceful because its objective is to create divergence."

Head Pint: "Yes, Fritz, everybody can aspire to have as big a voice as yours – word-punch above their weight, as it were. But the causes of our nemesis, societal divergence, go even deeper in our digital age…"

Tbc…

Session 3.4

Social Drinkers: "Are We Byting Off More Than We Can Chew?"

Texts, Highs, and Metascapes

"Calling all angels, we're sad and alone
We wandered too far, now it's time to come home;
We are falling …lost in the Garden."

- *"Calling All Angels", Eliza Gilkyson, 1995*

Geraghty's social drinkers are fearlessly ambitious but the road to peace is not an immaculate autobahn – as they accelerate into the fast lane, we wish them God-speed:

Cast of characters

- The Publican: Geraghty's owner
- The VC: Geraghty's funding source
- The social drinkers (whose personalities match their drinks): Head Pint, Slow Pint, Shandyman, Double Red Bull, Glass of Cab, Jameson with a Splash, exotic cocktail drinks, Teetotal drinks, and a host of other favorites
- The Dead Viziers: long-dead philosophers, musicians, scientists, and statespersons – deadly wise men eager to advise

Geraghty's social drinkers voted on the world problems they wanted to solve.

World Peace topped the vote as the most important problem facing mankind.

Amid a bit of antic behavior and the somewhat patronizing advice of the Dead Viziers, the social drinkers surprisingly decided that music was the solution to World Peace, reasoning that music is harmony and harmony is peace.

The more they talked about it, the more they were convinced that music was the solution. But what type of music?

The social drinkers rolled up their sleeves and set about understanding the process by which music affects the emotions to arrange addictive, harmonious rhapsody.

As C-19 waxed and waned, Geraghty's had become a micro-Metaverse hosting social drinking problem-solvers both physically in pubs and virtually in homes and in scanned 3-D pub settings.

They wondered whether they could use the spacious capabilities of their Metaverse to further their goal of World Peace through music.

The challenges were many.

They needed to compose music that created limitless empathy and was unifying.

Even if they succeeded in composing unifying music, how could they ensure that everyone had access to it?

They were living in the time of The Great Societal Divergence - could they get the pendulum to swing back toward convergence?

Where there were going to be winners, there would be losers - if mankind was a winner with World Peace, there were others for whom World Peace was anathema: certain governments, corporations, the United Nations, the military/industry complex, and the hegemonists.

So, Geraghty's social drinkers could expect severe, well-funded pushback if they looked like they were succeeding...

They had heard about a mysterious music system in a far-away Irish county on the wild Atlantic. It broadcasted music during an annual Harmony Day that united its people in limitless empathy. The social drinkers were curious about the composition of this unifying music. The people there were said to be very friendly but guarded about the capabilities of their music system.

...

Were Geraghty's social drinkers tilting at windmills? Could music really save mankind? And if so, could they create that music? The road was long with many a winding turn that would lead them to who knows where?[36]

Schopenhauer: "Yes, no, no, Hell. You are all doomed and there's nothing you can do. It's all just bits of bytes flying away from you.

"Look out world - take a good look - what goes down here. You must learn this lesson fast and learn it well.

"This ain't no upwardly mobile freeway - oh no, this is the road to Hell!"[37]

Comments:

YL: Dominic: Prior to working on a project, your intriguing Post effectively lured me in (smile). Say, make my drink a Strawberry Margarita. In addition, I've selected Johnny Nash (1972), "I Could See Clearly" as my #1 choice in helping the world solve its ills.

---

[36] "He's My Brother", The Hollies, 1969
[37] "The Road to Hell", Chris Rea, 1989

Session 3.5

Life - A Software Program Designed by the Gods, Intermittently Derailed by Random Acts of Free Will

"In that direction", the Cat said, waving its right paw around, "lives a Hatter. And in that direction", waving the other paw, "lives a March Hare. Visit either you like - they're both mad."

"But I don't want to go among mad people", Alice remarked.

"Oh, you can't help that." said the Cat. "We're all mad here. I'm mad. You're mad."

"How do you know I'm mad?" said Alice.

"You must be", said the Cat, "or you wouldn't have come here."*

Head Pint, continuing: "Spending more and more time on social media, many people rely on them as their sole source for news. Celebrity opinion-leaders on social media are viewed as oracles."

Schopenhauer, dourly: "Opinions do not represent knowledge."

Head Pint: "True, Artie, but they influence people - with today's information overload, attention spans are limited. News comes in sound bites. How profound can you be using just 280 characters?"

Slow Pint: "All right. Bottom line – social media enable individuals to communicate different views with various levels of aggressiveness, creating the potential of hyper-polarization across society - increasing societal divergence in opposition to our pursuit of convergence toward World Peace."

Glass of Cab: "I suppose it could get very lonely trying to find a person who agrees with you."

Head Pint: "Isn't it ironic? For some, social media could be re-named anti-social media, literally."

Glass of Cab: "Hold on, that's a bit one-sided — how could we have survived the lockdowns of C-19 without the wonderful communication tools provided by social media?"

Head Pint: "Yes, honor is due. But now, we are experiencing a perfect storm - seeing societal polyfurcation because of ineffectual curation in social media, the brevity of micro-blogging, the opaque prioritization of search tools, and "spun" newsfeeds.

"Maybe, without realizing it, we are already dwelling in a quasi-Metaverse, surrounded by fictions. Is life just a software program? Are we in The Matrix?"

Pellegrino with a Twist: "That's very dark! Yet paradoxically, you just asserted that many people consume their news and information from social media - ergo, they must trust that the news is credible."

Head Pint: "Hah! I rest my case. Who's in charge of separating fact from fiction from opinion? When are the skeptics going to stand up? To me, many news items seem like press releases or mini-op-eds."

Bottle of Stout: "Bottom line: a preponderance of evidence supports your assertion of ongoing societal divergence. It means that we are facing stiff headwinds in our quest for World Peace. Maybe we can't reverse the tide — are we on a pintless - sorry - pointless mission?"

Slow Pint, ponderously: "A pintless quest would be pointless."

Head Pint: "Ahem, thanks for your sauntering, droll wisdom. Now, as to our solution: using music to create World Peace - you know, these days some young people call modern music 'TikTok lip-sync audio'[38].

Maestro Mahler: "Rubbish! Let there be songs to fill the air — see the ripple in still water when there is no pebble tossed nor wind to blow."[39]

---

[38] Patrick Freyne, Irish Times, October 2021

Pierre Teilhard de Chardin: "Mon cher Gustav, c'est très Zen - mais je ne sais pas de quoi vous parlez.

"Didn't we all agree that love is the essence of World Peace?

"Pour moi, the question of the day is: 'Where's the love in all of this?'"

Tbc...

*"Alice's Adventures in Wonderland", Lewis Carroll, 1865

Session 3.6

Romancing the Metaverse

"Virtual space, the ultimate frontier - to boldly go where no mind has gone before..."

- *The Metaverse Enterprise, 2021*

VC: "In layman's language, the Metaverse is a shared, 3-D, virtual world that augments the 2-D experiences of social media. It immerses users in a virtual world - instead of just viewing content, you are part of it.

"It allows our physical and digital lives to overlap. The digital side is limitless since there are no geographic constraints. Unbounded virtual space will be at your fingertips without any need for warp speed."

Shandyman: "So, I'll be immersed in a different place without moving? I can get full immersion without traipsing upstairs for my Friday bath?"

Publican, sotto voce: 'Thank God this is Saturday.' Out loud: "The Metaverse has pluses and minuses that we need to understand. Inventive people will go in directions where no man has gone before. There'll be unintended consequences.

"Promoters of the Metaverse envision its users working, socializing, collaborating, and playing - everything from virtual concerts to conferences to trips around the world."

---

[39] "Ripple", Grateful Dead, 1970

Slow Pint: "How will the Metaverse affect Geraghty's quest for World Peace?"

Publican: "Well, I am proud to say that Geraghty's represents the first working Metaverse. We are in it!

"On the positive side for our quest, our Metaverse should be helpful for broadcasting our yet-to-be-composed Peace Anthem - everyone will be able to attend virtually."

Slow Pint: "Yes, I heard about plans for Metaverses that focus on music – virtual DJs, and virtual concerts with famous pop star and bands playing in fantastical landscapes."

Publican: "Also, the Metaverse can unleash the collective power of community: mobilizing members to solve global social problems, much as we do now.

"However, the Metaverse has the potential to accelerate the current societal divergence by amplifying the negative aspects of social media."

Flaming Red Cosmo - cascading red hair, color-coordinated rose-rimmed spectacles: "Our Pub Metaverse is eco-friendly - less global warming because there will be less commuting to local pubs."

Slow Pint, perking up, to Cosmo: "I like your style! Do you come here often? What's your star sign?"

Cosmo: "How retro! I've always wanted to meet a superannuated astromancer."

Slow Pint, unruffled by the whiff of faint praise: "Miss Cosmo, may I ask what your birthstone is?"

Cosmo, blushing: "Why, ruby, of course. My name is Mars after the red planet."

Slow Pint: "Hold on - isn't my name supposed to be Mars and yours Venus? Aren't we supposed to talk past each other?"

Cosmo, waving her empty glass: "Isn't that what we've been doing? I like the color red, so I'm going to call you Rory. Let's tighten up our communications: Ruaidhrí, a chara[40], can I ask you to order another one for me, please?"

Slow Pint: "Copy that. It would be my cosmic pleasure, Miss Mars."

Ailey, appearing out of nowhere: "Here's your smoking Cosmo!"

Slow Pint: "You're a mind-reader!"

Ailey, matter-of-factly: "All good bartenders have ESP."

VC: "Enough dalliancing! Let's get back on topic..."

Tbc...

Session 3.7

The Cost of Colonizing the Infinite Virtual Space of the Metaverse Is Limitless,

Beyond All but the Mega-Tech Companies

"We don't need your money, money, money
We just wanna make the world dance
Forget about the price tag...

Why is everybody so serious?
Acting so damn mysterious…

We need to take it back in time
When music made us all unite."

"Price Tag", Jesse J, 2011

Publican: "Society is moving to the next iteration of the Internet, Web 3.0. The boundless, 3-D Metaverse is part of it. Fitting out this space

---

[40] Rory, my friend

will be enormously expensive. There are development costs, infrastructure investments, and operating costs."

Slow Pint: "Hold it right there! Am I sensing the rank stench of a cross-subsidy?"

Publican: "No need to upset your supreme languidity - the price of the pint in Geraghty's Pub Metaverse is sacrosanct.

"Now, the Metaverse saw a total of $10 billion of VC funding invested in 2021. Meta Platforms alone invested $10 billion to start the build-out of its Metaverse."

Head Pint: "By the way, the notion that Web 3.0 will end the monopoly of the tech giants is a pipedream. Technological lock-in will occur because no corporation is going to spend billions without protecting their investment - power will be centralized in non-interoperable Metaverse platforms."

Bourbon with Absinthe Rinse: "If that's true, are y'all fixing to build your privacy-by-design Pub Metaverse as a communitarian space all-the-while avoiding these mega-jousters?"

VC: "I believe so - to them, Geraghty's Pub Metaverse will look like an ant on an elephant."

Publican: "Well, we have a cost and speed advantage: our scope is limited and well-defined - solving world problems by linking crowds of social drinkers to whom we sell pub-hub services. Everything is in place except the advanced technology itself.

"We'll need to procure holographic devices for our Metanauts, real-time edge storage, 3-D one-to-one space scans, blockchain and non-fungible token (NFT) software, a consensus-seeking algorithm, and 5G networking. Maybe we'll even mint our own pub crypto."

Double Red Bull: "Will I have to wear an apparatus on my head? That would completely throw off my drinking cadence."

VC: "Don't worry - it will not be a VR set - it will be a pair of spectacles - very special spectacles, mind you - with the capability to reconstruct holograms."

Yellow Spot with a Rock: "Excuse me - what in tarnation is an NFT? Sounds like it could be nifty."

VC: "Ha-ha-ha. An NFT is a uniquely owned digital asset located on the blockchain."

Yellow Spot with a Rock: "I am no wiser..."

Flaming Cosmo: "I don't like the sound of that algorithm - aren't algorithms causing lots of the troubles in social media and search engines in Web 2.0?"

Slow Pint: "My dear Mars, I wouldn't worry - this algorithm is different. Since we will have thousands of social drinking problem solvers, we need an algorithm to extract a consensus view based on their un-terse words of wisdom."

Head Pint: "Meanwhile, our Metaverse constitution - which is an extension of our pub precepts and principles of non-analytical behavior - will mandate transparency, privacy, and individual ownership of personal data per the stated aspirations of Web 3.0."

VC: "OK. Let's get down to brass tacks - how much capital do you need to raise?"

Publican: "I'd suggest that you sit down before I answer..."

Tbc...

Session 3.8

VC: "For a Few Dollars More?"

Publican: "No, I Will Need a Fistful of Dollars."

Metanauts: "Us Too. Our AR Devices and Virtual Travel Paraphernalia Don't Come Cheap."

"But I don't care too much for money - money can't buy me love."

- Beatles, 1964

Publican to VC, continuing: "My Metaverse business plan forecast says that we will need a mere $750 million of fresh capital. I'd suggest a 2X step-up to a pre-money of $33 billion - remember the good news: unlimited growth breeds unlimited valuations!"

VC: "Whew! That's the third round of financing in six months! And it's beaucoup dollars."

Publican: "Well, our customer base is exploding. If you want to pass, there are others very interested in jumping into this round - it's a steal at $33 billion!"

VC, quickly interjecting: "No, no, no, no...we'll do our pro-rata of $675 million - it's only right - after all, we are a social fund and Geraghty's Pub is definitely social.

"But, let me ask you: why must we buy Augmented Reality devices for our current 750 virtual social drinkers? Each holographic device costs about $500, plus, with the number of social drinkers growing so rapidly, it will cost a fortune to outfit all of them."

Publican: "Right on all counts, with one exception. We have five pub-hubs now, each supporting about 200 social-drinking problem-solvers, 75% of whom are virtual.

"Our Pub Metaverse is growing at warp speed. We are forecasting 10,000 problem-solvers by 2022, 100,000 by 2023 and 1,000,000 by 2025.

"Here's the one exception: we won't be giving the devices to our social drinkers. In return for their efforts to save mankind, we'll license the devices for free while we retain ownership. What have they got to lose? They'll become captive customers of Geraghty's!

"Remember, the more social drinkers, the more drink and meal deliveries, pub emulation services, pub workspace rentals, and pub fashion - real or 'skins' - we'll sell."

VC: "But can we really own our Pub Metaverse? It's a lot of money to invest without a solid ownership title."

Head Pint: "We are going to NFT all of our Pub's digital infrastructure to protect our intellectual property."

VC: "If you say so! Now, what about my ultimate liquidity event - how and when do I exit and realize a return on my massive investment? I can't stand the thought of an IPO in 2025. It seems a very long way away, and who knows what the tax situation will be by then."

Publican to VC: "So, you want me to come up with a plan for a future liquidity event that allows you to exit and realize your investment return.

"Let me pose a question to my very smart social drinkers: imagine if our Metaverse were to become a country with citizen Metazens. Remember, Metaverses already bypass physical geographic boundaries."

VC: "What's that got to do with my liquidity event?"

Publican: "Patience - in the fullness of time, I will provide you with a possible scenario, but I need to start with that question..."

Tbc...

Session 3.9

Countrifying the Metaverse

Metanauts: "We Are Virtually a Spacey Nation"

"The convergence of discourse and object, virtual and physical, mind and body, is what makes us human."

- *Jorge Carrión, "Against Amazon and Other Essays", Biblioasis, 2020*

Publican, continuing: "Let's suppose Geraghty's decides to "countrify" its Pub Metaverse - not as a game, but for real - call it the Pub Meta-Nation."

Head Pint: "Well, isn't our current mode of building a community of like-minded world-class problem-solvers akin to nation-building? Look, what does Geraghty's Pub's brand represent? First and foremost: solutions to save mankind. For example, we aim to be the first to create World Peace using music as our enabler. So, our brand would seem to port perfectly to a new meta-nation whose mission is to save the world and whose citizens are cosmopolites.

"It's an extraordinary concept - our own meta-nation-state. The national anthem could be our yet-to-be-composed 'Peace Rhapsody'!"

Flaming Cosmo: "Hmmm... I thought we agreed to call it the Earth Anthem.

"No matter, here's a thought - isn't Web 3.0 supposed to set users free - to put them in control of their domain? Instead of Big Tech making money selling users' data, couldn't our Metazens of the Pub Meta-Nation NFT their personal data? We could create our own 'national' pub-crypto, enabling entrepreneurial users to make money for themselves rather than for Big Tech in our crypto economy."

PM Lee Kuan Yew: "Perhaps the new nation's Metazens could own a share of meta-nation's digital 'common-land', the virtual acres - call them v-acres, like the land-held-in-common of a condo community."

Slow Pint: "I get it. We are not in the business of creating a colonial empire based on taking over land that somebody else owns. Our meta-nation creates altogether-new 'land' - like Jumeirah Island and The World Islands in Dubai - and then builds our infrastructure on this created 'land'. This would be similar to the strategy that the open-source DAO[41], Decentraland, now offers in its user-owned virtual world. For example, in June 2021 Sotheby's created a digital replica of its New Bond Street headquarters in London as a virtual gallery in Decentraland to show digital art."

PM Lee Kuan Yew: "Since you are aiming to save mankind without reference to indigeneity, people could become Metazens from anywhere across the globe - cosmopolitans, if you will.

"Governance could be democratic, even communitarian - perish the thought! I've always believed that a feared leader with a hatchet is the way to go, but I will bow to your naïve democratic ideals."

Publican: "I'd even go one step further, PM Elky - Geraghty's social drinkers could own shares in Geraghty's Pub's Metaverse business itself. They could share in the upside in return for their collaborative problem-solving solutions. It seems only fair."

"For governance, we'd need to draft a new Constitution for our meta-nation - we've laid a good foundation with our pub precepts and principles of operation."

Slow Pint: "Whew!"

Cosmo: "I'll second that Whew and add a Crikey!"

---

[41] Decentralized Autonomous Organization

Slow Pint: "Oh, do you come from a land down under
Where women <like you> glow and men blunder?[42]"

Session 3.10

Outfitting for the Metaverse Safari:

Into the 'Wild'

"Born to be wild...
Get your motor runnin'
Head out on the highway
Looking for adventure
In whatever comes our way."

-   *"Born to Be Wild". Steppenwolf, 1968*

Slow Pint: "Tell me more about the infrastructure required to make our Metaverse work."

Publican: "All right. First, let's talk about Metaverse access. You enter the Metaverse using virtual and augmented reality headsets, or new, personal appliances with embedded chips.

"3-D Augmented Reality (AR) can be layered on top of physical space using holographic technology - glasses with waveguides that reconstruct the hologram transmission packets. AR is better than VR because interacting online becomes much closer to the experience of interacting in person as holograms create more realistic virtual presences.

"Holography can help us observe body language, assuming the holograms exactly mimic the real person's behavior, and that the behavior is not faked.

"Second, Metaverses have massive storage requirements."

---

[42] "Down Under", Men at Work, 1981

Slow Pint: "Won't everything be in The Cloud? Isn't that the domain of Metaverses?"

Publican: "No, latency would be an issue - to create a non-juddering Metaverse, we will need to use a combination of local and cloud storage. Distributed storage in edge devices will be important for clear, real-time representations."

Slow Pint: "I sometimes experience the judders in the pub."

Publican: "Hmmm...third, the Metaverse will need massive bandwidth for real-time updating of 3-D images. 5G has a critical role to play.

Fourth, we'll need to construct 1-to-1 3-D scans of real physical spaces for insertion into the Metaverse.

"Why? Because while some social drinkers will travel physically to our pub-hubs, some social drinkers will prefer to stay in their home bars and some will travel as a hologram to the virtual pubs, the latter being 1-to-1 copies of the actual pubs.

"We will need 3-D scans of people's homes and the routes from their homes to the pubs to enable them to travel there virtually. The routes will be conceptually similar to Google Maps, but in 3-D - perhaps we can piggyback on the scans that autonomous cars use for navigation.

Glass of Sherry: "Doesn't that go against our privacy principles? It'd be quite intrusive."

Publican: "Well, we'll offer it on an opt-in basis and limit it to the home snugs. And the addresses and virtual routes would be visible only to the homeowners."

"Fifth, to enable commerce in the Pub Metaverse, we will need to use blockchain for storing our digital assets as NFTs and executing commercial transactions. It seems to me that pub crypto is a must.

"Lastly, new applications development will be very expensive initially until tools and building-block modules are standardized for 3-D. Then, we'll be limited only by our imagination. We will ensure IP protection for new applications using NFTs and compensate our app developers using crypto."

Bombay and Tonic Twist: "But we won't need this entire infrastructure at once, will we? I assume that our Metaverse will be rolled out in phases since the technology will get more complex the more Metaversal we become…"

Tbc…

Session 3.11

The Metaverse Is No Country for Old Men

Ko-Ko: "There is beauty in extreme old age —
Do you fancy you are elderly enough?
Information I'm requesting
On a subject interesting:
Is a maiden all the better when she's tough?"

Katisha: "Throughout this wide dominion
It's the general opinion
That she'll last a good deal longer when she's tough."

- *"The Mikado", Gilbert & Sullivan, 1885*

Publican: "Generally speaking, it is likely that in the near future there will be a phased roll-out of multiple "infant" Metaverses, including Geraghty's, probably none will be interoperable but all using standardized blockchain and NFT software.

"Currently, Metaverses are mostly stand-alone or "moated castles". We don't know if or when some of these might ultimately be linked to each other to create a meta-Metaverse."

Shandyman: "Not everyone will be able to afford the full Metaverse experience. Won't there be different classes of Metaversal immersions with different prices? Premium 3-D travel and gatherings using holograms will obviously cost the most; avatar meetings will be at a lower price-point; and lastly, bargain-basement Zoom meetings as we do currently."

Carafe of Mouth-Puckering Pinot Grigio: "So, you are saying that there will be 'haves' and 'have-nots'. Participating in the Metaverse won't be cheap - the well-off will be able to afford deep immersion, but others may be economically constrained to videos, avatars, or the WWW.

"Could we be looking at a split among our social drinkers and, for that matter, populations as a whole, between full-immersion people and those who can only afford to be toe-dippers?"

Publican: "Not at Geraghty's - everybody will be outfitted with the same gear at the same time. The last thing we want to do is add to the current divergence of society - exactly the opposite of our World Peace goal. We will not create a caste system of the 'haves' versus the 'have-nots'. However, this societal tiering will likely happen in other Metaverses.

"All of our social drinkers will be upgraded for free as we implement phased releases of more sophisticated devices and increased levels of immersion in our Pub Metaverse - our social fund VC was in alacritous agreement."

VC (sotto voce): "Alacritous? I've never felt less eager in my life...this is going to cost a fortune!"

Smathán of Jameson 18: "I can imagine that gamers will segue effortlessly_into the technology 'wild' of the Metaverse – it will be second nature to them.

"But what about us of the older generation who are not that conversant with the digital world? How will the digitally challenged participate in a digital society?

"Will we become outcasts left behind as the digital society accelerates away from us? Will we oldsters become dependent on geeks or our grandchildren for digital help?

"These days, young children are designing and creating their own micro-Metaverses using avatars downloaded free from the Internet. I am beginning to feel that I am from another planet - only last week, my own grand-daughter developed a Metaverse on her iPad!"

Publican: "Old man, your pint, sorry, point is well-taken. Given the connection and stability issues we have had with something as simple as Zoom, the Metaverse could be a nightmare for the uninitiated..."

Ko-Ko, doubtfully:
"Are you old enough to marry, do you think?
Won't you wait till you are eighty in the shade?
There's a fascination frantic
In a ruin that's romantic,
Do you think you are sufficiently decayed?"

Smathán of Jameson 18, serenely:
"To the matter that you mention
I have given some attention,
And I think I am sufficiently decayed."[43]

Session 3.12

Prospect of a Meta-Nation Creates Angst

Social Drinkers: "What Happened to the Nice, Quiet Pint of Yesteryear?"

"There is no safety this side of the grave."

- *Robert Heinlein, "Stranger in a Strange Land", Ace Pub., 1961*

Publican, turning back to the VC: "So, countrifying our Metaverse would enable us to crystallize your investment return soon.

"Upon becoming a meta-nation, Geraghty's would issue sovereign crypto bonds to buy-back your VC shares.

---

[43] "The Mikado", Gilbert & Sullivan, 1885

"Since numerous nations use bonds to finance their budgets, we'd be no different to the real world, except that our Metazens, unlike normal citizens, would share ownership of the meta-nation itself through their ownership in Geraghty's.

Lee Kuan Yew: "What a strange thought - a country owned by its citizens!"

Publican: "In return for this upside, and in the interest of avoiding an ineptocracy - that is, a conventional, entrenched government bureaucracy - Metazens would donate a portion of their time, say 10%, to the administration of the meta-nation."

VC: "Ailey, I don't feel so well - could you mix something soothing for my stomach?"

Keralan virtual social drinker: "Madam über-bartender, I'd recommend you tackle this Ayurvedically - but be careful with that devilishly indelible turmeric!"

Publican (sotto voce): "I love this - our Metaverse is borderless!"

Ailey: "Great idea, Sri Parveen. One Thiruvananthapuram honey-ginger shot coming right up with rubber-gloved-shaved, fresh turmeric - this should straighten out our VC in short order."

VC: "Great! Could you please go easy on the cayenne?"

Publican to VC, continuing: "Ahem, thank you for the remedy but I don't think we are at Code Level Red Pepper yet!

"Look, we don't have to countrify our Metaverse right this minute.

"And here's some heart-felt advice: I think you'd be mad to sell your ownership in Geraghty's golden gooseberry anytime soon - we're in for a great run for years to come. We're practically at breakeven already!"

VC: "Um - this whole complex scenario creating a meta-nation is a bit of a leap, isn't it? Plus, you're proposing to pay me out in crypto. As a VC, I deal in cold, hard cash. I am not in the business of taking even the slightest risk, as you know. You have succeeded in making the dreaded

IPO look reasonably attractive which, up until now, I would've said was impossible!"

Publican: "Hold on - you've only been in the deal for less than 12 months and your shares are already worth north of $300 million."

VC: "Yes, but in a choppy sea of uncharted crypto. Plus, I'm concerned about the colossal size of the future investment required to stand up Geraghty's digital meta-nation."

Slow Pint: "Sorry, guv, I agree with her. Isn't this all a bit too complicated? I come to the pub for a quiet, social pint and un-fanfared problem-solving.

"Do I really want to own a portion of a byzantine meta-nation and endure the stress of being a part-time administrator? Do I want to wear awkward, unfashionable spectacles that may interfere with the perfected rhythm of my drinking? Thanks, but no thanks!"

Hemingway Old Fashioned, Stiff: "<Sigh> Me, I've been trying to simplify my life…"

Double Red Bull: "Old men, haven't you heard of living dangerously?"

Publican: "Hmmm…Maybe countrifying isn't such a great idea after all…"

Omani virtual social drinker: "Before you decide, I would suggest that you have a glass of fragrant frankincense water…it will help you see clearly. I'm sure your parish priest has some."

Ailey: "That's a weird coincidence - I got some from Fr. Michael yesterday. I was going to burn it in the pub for its beautiful scent. Here - I've infused this glass of Ballygowan with frankincense particles."

Publican: "Delicious! I can see clearly now, the rain has gone - gone are the dark clouds that had me blind. Here is that rainbow I've been praying for. It's going to be a bright, sunshiny day!"[44]

---

[44]"I Can See Clearly Now", Jimmy Cliff, 1993

Chef Niamh na Prátaí[45]: "What a load of rubbish! What you need is a feed of my Cuinneog Farmhouse buttered, floury potatoes washed down with a pint of Guinness[46] It'll boost your IQ immediately but beware - it may also cause you to levitate a bit malodorously while making a small contribution to global warming...otherwise, you are welcome!"

Tbc...

Session 3.13

Oizys: "Won't the Metaverse Increase Today's Societal Divergence?"

Big Tech: "Don't Be Silly - Our Metaverses Are Solely Collaborative!"

Lotus-Eating Metazen: "Look, if I Have to Live in Meaninglessness, I'd Like It to Be My Own Meaninglessness!"

"Don't worry 'bout a thing,
'Cause everything little thing's gonna be all right."

- *Bob Marley and the Wailers, 1977*

"We gotta get out of this place,
If it's the last thing we ever do
Girl, there's a better life for you and me."

- *Eric Burden & The Animals, 1965*

---

[45] Chef Niamh (pronounced "Neeahv") of the Potatoes, Chapter 10, "Sumerian Vortex - Mayo Goes Mental", 2021
[46] "Sumerian Vortex - Mayo Goes Mental", 2021, page 82.

Publican: "We'll piggyback on the development work of Big Tech and even one nation that are hard at work creating Metaverses, its devices, low-latency storage, 3-D scans, and business models."

Double Red Bull: "As a gamer myself, I know that gaming companies are porting their products into Metaverses, cheered on by Nvidia."

Soju Neat: "My own South Korea has created a 'Metaverse Alliance' to build a national, mixed-reality platform and sort out the ethics and governance of virtual environments. Caveat emptor: we believe that a Metaverse computing platform is likely decades away."

Bottle of Old Vine Zinfandel, Decanted: "I've no doubt that the Metaverse will help social media corporations increase their attention-minutes - perhaps even convert them into hours - as customers enter into a "Life, the Movie" virtual ecology.

"We've already heard from the CEO of MugShot[47], and I quote: 'There's gonna be something after video, and it's gonna be much more immersive, and it's gonna be something that we can do throughout the day. I think if we're all spending a lot more time in the Metaverse, I think we're gonna care a lot more about our representation of identity. It's all about attention and connection.'[48]

'There is a tide in the affairs of a corporation which taken at the flood, leads on to fortune. Omitted, our voyage is bound in shallows and in miseries. On such a full sea we are now afloat. And we must take the current when it serves or lose our ventures.[49]'"

Jameson 18, Splash: "See? Mugshot is already planning to use tracking data for persistent, targeted advertising within the Metaverse. I doubt that it'll be an opt-in choice for users."

Salty Dog: "I call it surveillance capitalism!"

---

[47] "Sumerian Vortex – Mayo Goes Mental", March 2021
[48] "W3/Metaverse Chat", Interview by Gary Vaynerchuk, October 2021
[49] "Julius Caesar", William Shakespeare, 1599 (mostly)

Hendrick's & Tonic, Shave of Cucumber: "Alas and alack! As the Metaverse grows, society will likely splinter even more. Corporations intend to create an addiction to a 3-D virtual world just like the addiction to social media. The goal will be to entice users to emigrate from real life and dwell for extended periods of time in an exciting always-on virtual world of their own making."

Friedrich W. Nietzsche: "That shouldn't be too difficult to accomplish for Big Tech. Life is tough. I once said that what does not kill you makes you stronger, but I was medicated at the time. Remember, when you gaze long enough into a Metaverse, the Metaverse also gazes into you."

Head Pint: "Herr Professor, you are a master at doling out oracular inferences. Now, how many times can a man turn his head and pretend that he just doesn't see? The answer, my friend, is blowing in the wind; the answer is blowing in the wind."[50]

Bottle of Stout: "Bottom line: the Metaverse looks like a much bigger business opportunity than social media and potentially more disruptive."

Slow Pint: "Can you name names? What companies are involved in the Metaverse?"

Double Red Bull: "No real surprises here: Meta, Microsoft, Apple, Nvidia, Sony, Amazon, Disney, Qualcomm, and T-Mobile. Also, crypto- and NFT-related businesses. Plus, there is a myriad of start-ups.

"For example, this year Microsoft will release a mixed reality set of products with holograms and virtual avatars for retail commerce and workplaces."

"And the CEO of Meta has said that the Metaverse is the future of social connections and is critical for capturing younger audiences."

Tbc...

---

[50] "Blowin' in the Wind", Bob Dylan, 1963

Comments:

HG: If half of humanity is living in Metaverses will the other half have to do all the work? Eloi and Morlocks? Help!

DG: Now, that's an interesting question about the labor force:

First of all, the Eloi (The Time Machine) never lift a finger - the word "work" is not even in their vocab. Their life is 100% leisure until they become dinner for the dreaded Morlocks. Modern-day Eloi-citizens of the physical world are expecting to survive at their leisure on their guaranteed minimum income provided by the government.

Secondly, the Metazens believe that they are at work virtually all the time and come back to the physical world solely for R&R.

So, we have a serious problem: if most of the physical citizens are the Eloi, and the other half are Metazens who engage only in virtual work, there is nobody left to do the actual work.

Perhaps we can enlist Artificial Intelligence to do the work? I am told that AI handles almost everything these days...

Plus, let me see if Deep Thought will take a second question (without lengthening its time frame) and I will hopefully get back to you with an answer in the fullness of time...

Session 3.14

Will the 3-D Metaverse Be Another Nail in the Coffin of 2-D Reading and Writing?

*"Lonely days are gone, I'm a-goin' home
My baby, just-a wrote me a letter."*

- *"The Letter", Boxtops, 1967*

*"Dear Sir or Madam, will you read my book?
It took me years to write, will you take a look?...
It's a thousand pages, give or take a few...
And I wanna be a paperback writer,
Paperback writer."*

- *"Paperback Writer", Beatles, 1966*

Bespectacled Irish Coffee, Floated Chilled Cream, stowing a book in his satchel: "(Sigh) I can imagine a book-Metastore where you'll explore shelves virtually and open books with their own micro-Metaverses tailored to their content. Maybe Amazon will jump into that as its first foray into its Metaverse? Didn't it recently decide to close all of its physical bookstores?"

Metaverses: "We have met the books and they are us!"

Weiner Kaffe mit Schlag[51], nodding: "Mein Freund, es ist eine Tragödie[52] - physical bookstores are becoming anachronisms - in the Metaverse, you won't even need to read the written word - you'll be immersed in a 3-D video with a soundtrack! Eventually, writing will become obsolete - pencil, pen, ink, and blotting paper companies will go the way of the fountain pen.

---

[51] Viennese coffee with fresh-whipped, full cream
[52] My friend, it is a tragedy.

"What will we do in the Kaffeehäuser[53] if we have no books to discuss?

"Even today, how many write by hand in a paper notebook? I've been informed that there are young people who can't write cursively ('are you telling me that those squiggles mean something?') - instead, they print letters when they write - it's a grave new world..."

Double Red Bull: "Give me a break, altmodisch Österreicher[54]! I say to you: show me, don't write to me! Reading and writing are so quaint, so yesterday, so 2-D - a very inefficient way to communicate - so much unnecessary effort involved. We should replace these time-wasting middlemen with voice and vision! Micro-blogging was a move in the right direction but even 280 characters is a bit much. I'm a big fan of sound bites!"

Publican: "And so are we, Your Hyperness, or hadn't you noticed between twitches? By pub rule, our social drinkers are forbidden to write anything down during the problem-solving sessions or bring any written analysis into the pub - with the one exception: those over 75 can use the back of one standard-sized beer mat as an aide-mémoire."

Tbc...

Session 3.15

Orwell: "It's 1984 + 38!"

Bavarian: "Will the Metaverse Become a Mettwurst?"

"I've been livin' - livin' - on a dead-end street,
I've been askin' - askin' kindly - everybody I meet,
Insufficient data coming through."

- *"Sweet Talkin' Woman", Electric Light Orchestra, 1978*

Pessimist's Requiem with Orange Peel: "The Metaverse world sounds very Orwellian - the platform provider can watch everything we do

---

[53] Coffee-houses
[54] Old-fashioned Austrian

there. Can't we cover our tracks or even lay false trails? Create an alter ego or a false-flag legend?"

Double Red Bull: "Could overwhelm the tracking algorithms by injecting teeming, spurious data into our murmuration?"

Publican: "Don't you already do that every day? My friend, you're nothing if not spurious.

"The evolution of digitization isn't on our side. The Internet allowed marketers to study where customers moved their mouse or looked on a screen. Social media allows marketers to tailor ads to personal behavior as traced on their platforms.

"Some devices even track eye movements - mind you, cross-eyed oglers are impervious. Trysters are paranoid - their cars and phones are beacons - they know they're leaving an indelible, virtual trail behind them."

Barking Spider: "The only way you should go into the digital world is with eyes wide shut!"

Publican: "Very droll! Look, the new Web 3.0 Metaverse is searchable, clickable, and machine-readable. Digital records of users' behavior and interactions will be collected via wearable devices. These records underpin the Metaverse's business model - without it, the model doesn't work."

Publican: "What a boon to marketers! Self-reinforcing commercial suggestions and ads can be customized based on a person's data murmuration. Individual Metazens will like and feel comfortable with everything presented because the platform will achieve close to a 100% match with the individual's preferences and convictions."

VC: "That's very efficient - it'll save me a lot of dithering time."

Freud: "Yes, true, but there are some serious downsides. Since no contrary alternatives will be presented, discovery, learning, thinking, analysis, and healthy skepticism will be negatively impacted. Individuals will be hearing what they want to hear and seeing what they want to see."

Herbert George Wells: "So, Ziggy - there'll be no inconvenient truths. Virtual living will be effortless. Congenial thoughtlessness will reign. This reassuring comfort will create a preference for the unreal, virtual world and lead to alienation from the real, physical world."

Neuroscientist: "True and, heavens to Betsy, once warehoused in the Cloud, data murmurations will never be forgotten!"

> The year 2067:
>
> Jitter Juice: "Your honor, the event under question happened a long-forgotten 45 years ago - I've grown up into a responsible citizen since then."
>
> Longevitated Judge: "Sorry, my son, nothing's long-forgotten anymore - the court has the data right here at its fingertips. I'm projecting your aforementioned subversive dream holographically and entering it into the record. I must say that it seems quite damning - but of course, you're innocent until the data is verified."

Roll-of-the-Dice Whiskey and Orange: "So, bottom line, you're all saying: 'what happens in the Metaverse won't necessarily stay in the Metaverse."

Tbc...

HG: Will I own my Metaverse, or will it own me? Confusing!

DG: That's a very deep, philosophical question - a head-scratcher. Let me get back to you on that. It may make take a while - I will have to consult Deep Thought, and you know what he's like - a million years one way or the other is nothing to him - it took him 7.5 million years to answer the previous question, and that question was nowhere near as difficult as the one you pose about the Metaverse - if I remember correctly, the previous question was: "what is the meaning of life?"

Session 3.16

The Metaverse: Mind-Reader *Par Excellence*

"I've looked at life from both sides now
From win and lose and still somehow
It's life's illusions I recall
I really don't know life at all."

- *"Both Sides Now", Joni Mitchell, 1966*

Neuroscientist, nursing her Mellow Mango Ω-3: "Recording data on where you go and the decisions you make in the Metaverse is just the tip of the iceberg. It'll also be possible to track your body movement, physiological responses and, eventually, even your thoughts."

Descartes: "What! And I believed that there was absolutely nothing in my power except for my thoughts! If I can't think, I won't be."

Hume: "Look, you're overthinking this - just walk away René, you won't see them follow you back home.[55]"

Neuroscientist: "Brain-computer interfaces (BCIs) will provide another way to access the Metaverse. They will be worn on the head like headphones or work through eyeglasses or wrist-bracelets. The BCI technology will track brain wave patterns and deduce thought processes through machine learning. A direct link to someone's brain would open a whole new vista of luscious, primary-source data to be collected and exploited."

Flaming Cosmo: "I don't like the sound of that at all! Will we need to firewall or encrypt our private thoughts in our brain: 'thank you, doctor, can I have my neurons scrambled, please'? It sounds like the Thought Police could make hay in the Metaverse. Worse - could the communication direction be reversed, and manipulative thoughts injected into our brains?"

---

[55] "Walk Away, Renee", Four Tops, 1967 (adjusted)

Freud, sipping a Monkey Brain: "There could also be inadvertent psychological effects - we know that people store virtual reality experiences in memory. They can feel that they carried out some action in the past even though they did not do it physically. How will our minds determine what was real? It'll be like the morning after: 'Surely I didn't do that last night!'"

> Plaintiff in witness box, pointing: "God's honest truth - I am sure it was that blackguard, your honor - I saw him do it!"

> Her Honor: "I'm afraid we'll have to do a brain trace to verify that, young man - don't worry, it won't hurt a bit..."

Neuroscientist: "And it's not just privacy, the potential for 'brainwashing', and mental stability that we'll need to worry about - there are also possible harmful physical effects.

"If we're sensing the virtual world and the real world at the same time in the Metaverse, how will the brain handle locational indeterminacy? Will its body-balance and motor functions be confused? Our motor-cortex could sense body movement without actually sending movement signals. What becomes of consciousness without a physical mooring?

"Wearers of AR devices for extended periods have reported motion-sickness and nausea - just like astronauts' experience in zero-gravity space. Metazens could have problems reentering the physical world after a long stay in virtual space."

Schopenhauer: "Mmmm - this is all exquisitely pessimistic."

Double Red Bull: "I have a question - if I take a rollercoaster ride in the Metaverse, will I feel doubly nauseous?"

Publican: "Strewth! Get a hold of yourselves, would you? You're all losing your muffins..."

Tbc...

Comments:

YL: I'm with the "Flaming Cosmo." Please notify me whenever they began scrambling our "Neurons?" (LOL) I'll be second in line. And the Plaintiff sounds awfully shady!

DG: HiYa Yo, the doctor is juggling some dopamine-related sunny-side-up neurons first and he'll get to your scramble in a jiffy. Re the plaintiff - you are right - I don't think this will be the last time we'll see him in court...

The brain-trace results are back, and it verifies that the plaintiff is hair-brained - you were right on the money. If he had half a brain (!), he'd try to stay out of trouble.

YL: By the way, I'm also going to consider the super concoction as my 4th vaccine (excluding the flu shot). And the plaintiff saying, "I saw him do it!" That's classic! 😄

DG: 'Super concoction': I assume you mean the Flaming Cosmo? Even in moderate doses, it's guaranteed to inoculate you against all viruses.

Session 3.17

Lost in the Metaverse:

Nur der Kuckuck Weiß, Wie Man Rauskommt*

"I am... I cried
I am... said I
And I am lost, and I can't
Even say why."

- *"I am, I Said", Neil Diamond, 1971*

*Only the cuckoo knows how to escape

Having concluded his much-lauded, tuneful yodeling, Freud sipped his Almdudler and his brow furrowed: "User addiction is a concern in the development of the Metaverse. We've already learned about Internet and social media addiction disorder, known colloquially as IS-MAD.

"Video gaming and metaversing over a prolonged period can have mental repercussions, causing depression and anxiety. As an aside, binge-dancing the Viennese waltz can have the same effect. Seriously, China has gone so far as to ban young people from spending more than three hours per day gaming and prohibits their gaming on the weekends.

"The Metaverse enables what I have dubbed 'metarsis' - a purging of strong or repressed emotions coupled with a repudiation of the responsibilities of living - an escape from real life into la vida loca.

"Metazens can 'live' in this always-on digital world by creating their personal domain. Getting there will be a lot easier to achieve than space travel, sailing to an uninhabited island, or dealing hallucinogens in the hard streets of the inner city - you can escape while sitting in an armchair in your living room."

Slow Pint: "Hold on - there are circuit-breakers that force addicts to leave the Metaverse periodically. One can't live continuously in the Metaverse without fuel and sleep - plus people will need to use a bathroom! At Geraghty's, we enforce traditional licensing hours for problem-solving sessions and ban, on the honor system, any extra-curricular world problem-solving outside of pub hours."

Freud: "Yes, but circuit breakers by themselves are not enough. In personal domains, everything will be congruent with the domain-owner's ego and preferences. The Metazen will always be right - pesky disagreers can be excluded. There will be unintended consequences - how many people can one find who will agree 100% with each other - that'd be unhuman, wouldn't it? So, the potential to create loners alienated from social interactions is high.

"Severe cases will lead to a new mental illness - 'Digititis' or D-22 - like a 'Master of the Universe' syndrome."

Friedrich W. Nietzsche: "Nonsense! My overman will have finally arrived...he who has organized the chaos of his passions and given style to his character. Aware of life's terrors, he will affirm virtual life without resentment.[56]"

Björn Tooby Wild Turkey: "On the positive side, there will be no homelessness anymore. Since virtual space is limitless, one will always be able to find a home in the Metaverse. Big cities will be able to create gentrified, virtual homeless shelters!"

Freud: "Herr Wild, hello? Anybody <ahem> home? Won't the homeless be physically still there while virtually not there? Are you all there yourself?"

Tbc...

Comments:

HG: As ever, this is all very informative. Will prepare me for a safe entry into the metaverse. If such a thing is possible?

DG: Entry is the easy part - re-entry from the zero-time Metaverse (as contrasted with zero-gravity) of virtual space to earthly physical space could be a challenge! Especially if licensing hours are over...one might have to drive to an unpatrolled shebeen in Glencullen for a restorative pint...

HG: I know that shebeen - it is Johnny Fox's - I will go up there for a remedy after I exit from the Metaverse.

DG: I'll raise my remedy to your remedy when the time comes!

---

[56] "On the Genealogy of Morals", Friedrich Wilhelm Nietzsche,1887

Session 3.18

The Next Pandemic: Digititis-22

It's a Common-Source Outbreak Created by Web 2.0

Super-Spreader: Web 3.0

Vaccine: Live Music

*"Don't it always seem to go
That you don't know what you've got 'til it's gone?"*

- *"Big Yellow Taxi" Joni Mitchell, 1970*

Voice of Reason Double IPA: "Here's what I don't get - if social media and Big Tech corporations were truly social, shouldn't they be helping to solve mankind's biggest problems rather than spending tens of billions creating alternative realities?"

Publican: "Vordi, doff those rose-colored glasses.

"Big Tech businesses' primary stakeholders are their shareholders and management. Solving mankind's problems is lower in priority, unless the solutions drive profits, that is, attention-minutes.

"Alas, world peace doesn't drive attention-minutes. In fact, it's its opposite - divisiveness - that racks them up. Plus, Metazens promising massive attention-minutes represent the cream of the market crop for them. Anti-social media, microblogging, gaming, and the Metaverse will foster the mental Digititis-22 pandemic that Ziggy Freud alluded to."

Probiotic Mango Lassi: "You mean - we are just going to substitute D-22 for C-19, both of which can create isolation, device addictiveness, and mental problems?"

Head Pint: "Look, the Metaverse will not be 100% benign, nor 100% commercial, nor 100% collaborative. It will provide a platform for a broad mix of businesses, do-gooders, don't-carers, manipulators, scammers, and criminals."

Vordi: "So, the Metaverse is being portrayed as collaborative, like social media were initially, but it could morph into a multi-headed Hydra, exacerbating the ongoing divergence of society as people head into the virtual world to escape life and its challenges and become addicted to unreality.

Publican: "Yes, but we are not completely innocent ourselves - aren't we at Geraghty's Pub Metaverse promoting addiction too?"

Slow Pint: "Hold on a minute - be fair! We want the addiction not to be about escape from life, but about the pleasures of intuition, wondering, discovering, and healthy skepticism, all to be put to work creating solutions that benefit mankind. Our work, even if a bit obsessive, is congregational, not escapist!"

Friedrich W. Nietzsche: "Isn't there a huge contradiction? Don't people know that there's no escape from life? Even if they immerse themselves in a virtual world, they will still be with themselves! The answer's simple - amor fati![57] All together now: Say Yes to Life!

"We've come so far, so fast, but somewhere back there, that same small town is in each of us. This cannot be the end of the innocence.[58] A peace like ours is peace that's hard to find. How could we let it slip away? We've come too far to leave it all behind.[59]"

Publican: "Look - the cure for D-22 is music. Music unites, D-22 divides!"

Pythagoras: "I find your suggested cure harmonious."

---

[57] Embrace your fate.
[58] "The End of the Innocence", Don Henley, 1989
[59] "If You Leave Me Now", Chicago, 1976

Wagner: "Yes, the gaffer is right - music is the elixir of life. For World Peace, it creates limitless empathy and universal love; for loneliness - an always-available companion; and for hopelessness - collective confidence and resolve!"

Tbc...

Comments:

YL: Dom: I really liked the first question posed. And of course, the Publican's response was considered another classic (loose the rose-colored glasses). Yep!

DG: Thank you! I suppose it's not totally fair to ask Big Tech to do the U.N.'s job but the latter has not been impressive about fulfilling its primary mission: World Peace -- politicization, bureaucracy, and political correctness have a lot to answer for in that regard...we shall be hearing more about that sad state of affairs from Geraghty's' crowd-solvers.

Yes, the Publican seems to be questioning Vordi's ability to meet the exemplary standard of intuition expected from the social drinkers...I mean to say, is he really a Voice of Reason?

YL: Dom: Clearly, we shouldn't expect Big Tech(s) to primarily focus and shoulder the world's greatest challenges (hunger, homelessness, etc.). That would be considered unreasonable. However, since the masses significantly contributed to their wealth, growth, and success, they should feel obliged to do their fair share.

DG: Fair enough. Each could do their bit. Social media should invest more heavily in improving the curation of incivility - that would move the peace needle in right direction.

In general, spirited debate on social or microblogging platforms informs everyone and can bring us together peacefully in terms of a better understanding of the legitimacy of views that we may not agree with.

On the other hand, arbitrary, un-transparent, or ideology-based censorship and cancel culture do the opposite - they rile up people and thus divide us in an un-peaceful way. Free speech is the cornerstone of our culture [1]. The social and communications platforms need to up their game for this admittedly difficult-to-solve problem.

[1] I recently read a new book that's quite good on this topic (and for the most part, quite balanced too): "Free Speech", Jacob Mchangama, Basic Books, 2022

HG: Very thought-provoking as usual, the punters in Geraghty's Pub. How can we encourage ourselves to think of the Whole, as earthlings on one planet and not polarize into opposing extremes? Could the Metaverse somehow encourage holistic thinking?

DG Interesting idea. Unfortunately, there are a lot of disincentives to embracing a holistic world view (in a journey to the Omega Point). I worry that we're moving towards the Alpha Point!

For example, divisiveness pays off for (anti-)social media by creating more attention-minutes (emotion-intensive power-plays by individuals and tribes alienates people), politicians spread disinformation to cast honest questions in the worst possible light - 'you're with me or you're not' - creating polarization, and the military/industrial complex finds wars profitable.

Will-to-power is a very - ahem - powerful force. Will-to-profit is not far behind.

Digitization:

Personal devices inhibit F2F (face-to-face) communication - small example: how often do you see members of a families in a restaurant all looking down at their devices? People leave meetings to answer their iPhone?

I think the Metaverse, when it happens, could divide people further since they are moving away from F2F interactions. Plus, the platforms offering the Metaverse are sure to repeat the tactics they use now to increase attention-minutes - I expect that users will be "stickier" because of the higher intensity of 3-D immersion versus the 2-D experience on the WWW.

DG: LinkedIn told me I ran out of available characters for my reply - which is a nice way to say TMI! FYI, I have been drafting a very short book (<40 pp) about this, but it's been tough so far to synthesize the many different factors affecting whether we converge or diverge as a society or as humankind. Digitization is a very big factor, I think. Can it be used to unite? Yes, in theory, but the business objectives of the potential owners of Metaverse platforms will probably amplify divergence.

Session 3.19

The Metaverse Is the Ultimate Colonization -

But of the Mind, Not the Land

Meet the Mental Conquistadors

"This land is mine, but I'll let you rule
I'll let you navigate and demand
Just as long as you know, this land is mine
So find your home and settle in
Oh, I'm ready to let you in
Just as long as we know, this land is mine."

- *"This Land Is Mine", Dido, 2003*

Publican to VC: "The Metaverse could be a market worth $800 billion as early as 2024. Its growth prospects are limitless, just as digital space is. There is room for anybody that wants to participate.

Head Pint: "True - it is likely that multiple non-interoperable Metaverse platforms will co-exist, creating together a meta- Metaverse. So, there will be no 'THE Metaverse'."

"We've been told multiple times by Big Tech that 'no one company will own and operate the Metaverse.' Even South Korea has warned us that the Metaverse "is not a space that is monopolized by a single large company but instead one in which participants collaborate.""

Ti Punch: "Look, it's simple: the Metaverse is just an extension of the 'colonization' of the Internet by the major internet companies. Territory will be staked out - named colonies will be branded and flagged with logos in pursuit of corporate virtual hegemony. Speed will be essential in this land-grab and population-building since market share momentum will be difficult for slow-starting companies to overcome.

"It is like the empire-building based on the conquests of the Spanish Conquistadors, the Portuguese Colonial Empire, the British Empire, and the Dutch West Indies.

Jameson, Splash: "So, we can call it corporate imperialism!"

Ti Punch: "In the interest of speeding up their conquest of virtual space, Big Tech will give people tools to develop properties in their virtual colonies, digital highways, railways to travel to corporation-selected destinations and virtual towns. It will look and feel like the real world.

Freud: "Pshaw! You are looking at this the wrong way! This is not the same as the conquest of land or natural resources! Since it is our minds that travel in the Metaverse, it is about the colonization of minds with feel-good emotions. Temporary sovereignty over the mind to catalyze commerce and entertainment is the goal.

"Powerful tracking algorithms will be used to strip privacy and guilefully target tailored ads that resonate with individuals' needs and wants. The anticipatory excitement will trigger the brain's pleasure drugs: endorphins or dopamine creating feelings of pleasure, un-blighted happiness as the Metazens escape from life and government oversight. The happy brain drugs will be catalyzed in users creating addiction and increasing dwell-time.

"Eventually, BCIs that can read thoughts, potentially leading to the possibility of mind-control - the thought police won't be needed - thoughts will be directly controlled.

"The colonies in the virtual domain will be created by the most powerful "software armies" in the world, more powerful than government. They will be filled with phalanxes of "patriots" - Governments will be side-stepped by massive investment not in ships or troops, but by a software army.

"In the future, rival Metaverses will conduct commercial war against each other, competing for attention-minutes, or better, attention-hours.

"Colonies will be swapped, bartered, acquired, and conquered - an investment bankers bonanza.

Drink: "Since the superstructure of the Metaverses will be in The Cloud, cloud owners will see a ton of new business.

"Colonies will be swapped, bartered, acquired, and conquered - an investment banker's bonanza. Since the superstructure of the Metaverses will be in The Cloud, cloud owners will see a ton of new business."

Big tech already knows this. Amazon, Microsoft, and Google - together they have over 2/3 of the Cloud storage market. Oracle is jumping in. Edge devices manufactured by Meta and Apple and a few others will be gatekeepers. The supply of the required real-time computer chips will be controlled by Nvidia and the like. Carrier 5G services will be controlled by AT&T, Verizon and T-Mobile."

Metaverse real estate agent: "Yes sir, you want to buy real estate - I can help you - virtual or physical? Prices of virtual are spiking due to epic demand. I have 1-to-1 replicas of buildings, mansions, estates, beachfront properties, roads, towns, cities, counties, states, provinces, islands, and even countries."

Metaverse travel agent: "I see, madam, you'd like to visit The Valley of the Kings without having to ride a real camel? I'd recommend the top-of-the-line authenticity of our latest high-res optics."

Tbc...

Comments:

DG: I've just received a high-dudgeon message from the shop-steward of the United Brotherhood of Thought Police Workers - she is not amused, and she conveyed to me that, in her capacity as a Thought Professional, she does not appreciate any of my thoughts. In fact, she said my thoughts are uninteresting, even boring, without even a hint of subversiveness. Nevertheless, she is willing to go before a neutral tribunal to arbitrate the matter if the hearing is oral only.

YL: Dom: Accordingly, "The Thought Police" won't be needed? Wow! That's unheard of (lol). Will they be absorbed in some capacity? Or will they be laid off - searching for perhaps Postal or Transit opportunities? (a position requiring some type of self-defense mechanism).

YL: That'll be insightful (smile).

DG: Sadly, it wasn't as insightful as we'd hoped (smile). The shop steward went into the arbitration hearing with eyes wide shut. The hearing was a sight for sore eyes...the judge's ruling was out of sight - I mean sealed, sight unseen. In hindsight, I should've had the foresight to have known - it was in plain sight the whole time.

HG: The colonization of minds! I guess the current fake news deceiving all those who want to be deceived is an example already. Scary stuff. Hopefully there will be rebels for the truth.

DG: "...those who want to be deceived..." - that's an interesting take! Are we too indifferent or even too complacent to be skeptical, or do we just accept that we will never be told the straight skinny? Maybe it is just too easy to get our news "bytes" from our personal devices by simply taking the effort to lift a finger? Here's to rebels for truth!!!

Session 3.20

The Story So Far...

"Huh? There's a Story Somewhere in All of This?"

"Where Do We Come From? What Are We? Where Are We Going?"

- *Paul Gauguin, Tahiti, 1897.*

It has been suggested that the warp and weft **of** my weekly episodic narrative can be difficult to follow if a reader jumps in in the middle of the story, having missed a few preceding episodes. Mea culpa. There is method to my madness – no, really!

There is a plot, gauzy though it may seem. All of the seemingly unconnected threads will come together in a grand denouement – a culmination which only the cuckoo knows.

The story so far:

Geraghty's Pub had to close due to C-19. The cessation of its social drinkers' world problem-solving sessions was a massive loss for mankind.

The Publican decided to transubstantiate the pub into a virtual venue for his social drinkers using Zoom to create a proto-Metaverse. He approached a social fund VC and raised a stack of capital.

To make the virtual more real, Geraghty's decided to offer just-in-time trucked deliveries of fresh pints of porter and food deliveries via bicycled messenger boys from its physical pub to the doorsteps of its social-drinkers' homes.

This initial business strategy was so successful that Geraghty's decided to acquire additional physical pubs, creating a network of pub-hubs for its delivery services and virtual problem solving. The VC complied with another massive infusion of capital.

As C-19 restrictions decreased, Geraghty's pubs reopened their physical spaces and suitably distanced social drinkers reassumed their world problem-solving duties F2F.

The social drinkers decided to list and prioritize the important problems of mankind to be tackled. They were advised by a cadre of very wise Dead Viziers.

World Peace was the top vote-getter.

The social drinkers, strongly influenced by the Dead Viziers, decided intuitively that the solution to World Peace was obvious: music.

But what type of music?

Everyone knew that certain music could be transcendent, creating strong, spiritual, even euphoric emotions. If Geraghty's social drinkers could understand how emotions were derived as the brain processed music, perhaps they could design music that created universal empathy, thus enabling world peace.

Then they would need to find a way to broadcast the music to the entire world.

They heard about an ancient music system in County Mayo on the west coast of Ireland that created euphoria across its population during its annual Harmony Day. The Publican decided to visit Mayo to find out more...

It wasn't the most conducive time to achieve world peace. Societies seemed to be diverging into mono-viewpoint factions, and individual privacy was under attack. Shaking his head sadly, Dead Vizier Orwell decided to retitle his book 1984 + 38.

Opposition to World Peace reared its ugly head. Vested interests whose livelihoods depended on peacelessness – corporations, governments, bureaucrats, so-called experts, and the U.N. expressed pious concerns about peacefulness.

Could Geraghty's use music to create world peace within this fractious world? Or was the world headed for dystopia?

Did the Publican have a Plan B?

Tbc...

Comments:

RP: I can't imagine this wonderful tale coming to an apocalyptic end. My imagination tells me a solution will be found by the cuckoo!

DG: I have full faith and confidence that the cuckoo will find a suitable nest!

HG: Very helpful summary! Now we know exactly where we are. (Just where is that? I float in cyberspace ...)

DG: Great! You have already transcended, and you haven't even heard the music yet!

Topic #4

Anniversary Party

Session 4.1

Six-Month Anniversary Party for the Launch of Geraghty's Pub Metaverse

*"It was the best of times, it was the wurst <stet> of times;
it was the age of wisdom, it was the age of foolishness; it was the
epoch of belief, it was the epoch of incredulity; it was the spring of
hope, it was the winter of despair; we had everything before us, we had
nothing before us..."*

- *"A Tale of Two Cities", Charles Dickens, 1859*

Publican, white shirtsleeves rolled up, tricolor suspenders with pressed khakis: "Welcome to Geraghty's Pub Metaverse – our party is in full swing! I've invited all our Matazens to have a virtual drink with me and meet our social drinkers, known far and wide as the saviors of mankind. My Dead Viziers are here too and will provide us with some very wise chestnuts."

Hesse: "What a waste of time...my Glass Bead Game answers everything – there's no need for these superannuated wiseacres."

Publican: "Ahem, I'm not sure we are all of the same kidney. Moving on: to avoid any whiff of discrimination between physical and virtual presences, everyone needs to wear a mask - we have some very nice face 'skins' for the virtually fashion-conscious. No name tags are permitted in the interests of decorum but I'm sure you will all recognize our Dead Viziers who are, super-naturally, exempt from mask-wearing."

Dead Viziers: "Right, there are some advantages to being dead! For example, we don't need to knock, knock, knock on heaven's door to gain admittance."

Publican: "We've completed deliveries of fresh pints and other beverages to the virtual attendees who ordered them, and I see that those of you with your own home snugs are also well supplied. Excellent!

"You can see Geraghty's social drinkers behind me in the pub and I'm projecting holograms of myself, Head Pint right behind me, and our Dead Viziers into the ether to increase the personableness of the occasion – by the way, for those of you who are technology-challenged, holograms will not give you C-19 even if you walk right through them.

"And here's some splendid 3-D group holograms of our six cadres of social drinkers who are present physically at our other pub-hubs!"

...flickering screens full of odd assortments of happy heads, some with home-bars visible in the background... physical pub-hubs appearing as full as social distancing allowed... holographic projections filling the spaces between the physicals.

Publican: "Let's start with a meditation. Imagine a Silver Oak Cab, 1994 – can you remember? While you won't actually be able to taste it physically, your memory neurons should release a tincture of dopamine, just as fondly remembered music does.

"Imagine the intensity, mouthfeel, swallow density, and brilliant finish! I see that a few of you don't need any imagination – you are sitting on your home bar stool reverently swirling the inky elixir of a '94 Silver Oak from your personal stash in a massive glass, in anticipation of a full-sensory imbibement. We send you our envy."

Dead Viziers: "Well, we have no sense of taste anymore – and no dopamine swirls our brains – eternal happiness takes care of that need. All that's left is our imagination and memories, admittedly a bit hazy after all these years of drinking heaven's ambrosia."

Head Pint: "Hmmm...moving on: for those of you who won't drink anything except pulled porter..."

Tbc...

Comments:

HG: The eloquence of your barman and customers is dazzling! Very exceptional drinkers in that pub. Must be the Metaverse effect.

DG: The Metaverse moves in mysterious ways! The social drinkers and Ailey seem to become virtual wordsmiths!

Session 4.2

The Pub's Anniversary Party Continues...

Ailey Tries to Liven Up Things with a Drearily Named Drink

Einstein, Planck and Tesla Disagree; Pythagoras Feels Vindicated

Head Pint, continuing: "For those of you who won't drink anything except pulled porter, you'll be glad to hear that we have almost perfected holographic pints of Guinness – the head is a perpetual brilliant white – behold its sheer beauty - dazzling, really. However, we are struggling with how to add the bitter-sweet taste and its characteristic scent of old socks.

"Meanwhile, I'm delighted to announce that we've been able to duplicate the harmonious clinking of an ice cube in a smathán of Jameson 18."

Pythagoras: "I love harmonics!"

Über-Bartender Ailey: "I'm going to mix a round of virtual Lashing Rain cocktails (c.f. post: June 18, 2021) for everyone. They'll be accompanied by a virtual tropical rainstorm. Cheers!"

Publican: "Will you serve these with Tiki umbrellas?"

As we pan across the pubs and the virtual snugs, we come across various cameos:

Pericles: "I have composed a small encomium for our social drinkers: 'Ask not what you can do for your... sorry, wrong encomium. <throat-clearing, followed by mellifluous intoning> You should fix your eyes every day on the greatness of Geraghty's Metaverse as it really is, and should fall in love with it...

"When you realize our Pub Meta-Nation's greatness, reflect then on that what makes it great are social drinkers with a spirit of adventure, Metazens who know their duty, people who are ashamed to fall below a certain standard.

"If they ever fail in an enterprise, they make up their minds that at any rate our Meta-Nation should not find their courage lacking, and they give the best contribution that they can...'[60]"

PM Lee Kuan Yew: "What a load of rubbish! Fear is the best motivator - I have a hatchet and I will use it as needed."

Einstein: "As if! Never mind - I have discovered that time and its inverse are all we need to know - the essence of everything is vibration. Vibes are matter and matter is vibration.

"So, $E=mc^2$. The mass of Guinness multiplied by the speed of vibrant light squared is the energy imparted to the imbiber by the proverbial pint."

Planck: "Sorry, Bertie, the pint's energy is measured by the frequency of the light emitted by the white head of the pint multiplied by my constant - the correct formulation is $E = h\nu$."

Tesla, yawning: "Look, forget about old-news energy-matter relationships - I've a news flash about high voltage that is shocking."

Jameson with a Splash: "That's also old news - I've long heard that White Lightning gives you a healthy jolt."

---

[60] Loosely sourced from Pericles' "Funeral Oration", Thucydides (460 B.C. – 400 B.C.)

Maestro Mahler: "Servus an alle[61]! Talking about lightning – my monumental 5th symphony came to me in a flash - I heard ringing in the heavens."

Pythagoras, gratified: "Ah, so you heard my Music of the Spheres!"

Tbc...

Session 4.3

Pub Metaverse's Anniversary Party:

Nietzsche Makes an Amorous Advance

"Temptation, oh, temptation,
Were we, I pray, intended
To shun, what e'er our station,
Your fascinations splendid;
Or fall, whene'er we view you,
Head over heels into you?"

-   *Elsie, Lieutenant, and Point: "Yeoman of the Guard", Gilbert & Sullivan, 1888*

Friedrich W. Nietzsche: "I'd like to present a short poem in praise of Fraulein Cosmo – you remind me of my unhealthy admiration for my dear friend Cosima Wagner at the Villa Tribschen."

Wagner: "Yes, it was indecorous, to say the least, after all I'd done for you."

Friedrich W. Nietzsche, clearing his throat, to Cosmo: "So much depends upon a red wheelbarrow, glazed with rainwater, beside the white chickens.[62]"

---

[61] Dia dhaoibh do gach éinne!/Hello to all!
[62] "The Red Wheelbarrow", William Carlos Williams, 1883-1963

Cosmo: "Beg pardon? So, I'm a red wheelbarrow, am I? Not very flattering, except for the red part. Sounds like another unhealthy admiration!"

Friedrich W. Nietzsche: "No, wait - that didn't come out right - I have a better poem...

"Butterfly, my butterfly, I'll come home to you one day. Butterfly, my butterfly, wait for me - don't fly away."[63]

Slow Pint, hackles raised, talons flexing: "Butterfly? Don't you dare accuse my <ahem> our Cosmo of being a flittering butterfly with your plagiarized ditty - nothing could be farther from the truth. Let me tell you that I am the eagle, I live in high country - in rocky cathedrals that reach to the sky.[64]"

Friedrich W. Nietzsche: "Me and my Übermensch are not afraid of you. But wait, scratch that last poem, I have an even better one...

"I'm just mad about Cosmo, Cosmo's mad about me, I'm-a just mad about Cosmo, she's just mad about me. They call me mellow fellow. Quite rightly![65]

"Fraulein Cosmo, you also remind me of my vivacious Russian friend, Lou von Salomé. May I have the next dance - everybody knows I'm a great dancer!"

Flaming Cosmo: "Well, you certainly got around, didn't you, for a pallid philosopher! I'm very flattered, Herr Professor Mellow Fellow Friedrich, but you're too hairy for me - your moustache is fearfully flareful.

"Pardon me if I ask you to act upon your own words: 'There is one path in the world that none can walk but you. Where does it lead? Don't ask, walk!'"

---

[63] "Butterfly", Jim Ed Brown, 1972
[64] "The Eagle and the Hawk", John Denver, 1972
[65] "Mellow Yellow", Donovan, 1966

Slow Pint, coming up to flank speed: "Hear, hear! Take that hike, you preening, platitudinous Prussian! Tchüss, tchüss, scarper, skedaddle, Fritz! Shake a leg and go back to your lost loves. And take Dionysus with you, would you?"

Friedrich W. Nietzsche: "Bang bang, she shot me down; bang bang, I hit the ground; bang bang, that awful sound; bang bang, my lady shot me down.[66]"…

Cosmo, cozying up to Slow Pint: "So, you like the color red?"

Slow Pint, drinking pace accelerating way beyond his maximum allowable Reynolds Number of 2,000: "Let me just say that I've never seen you looking so gorgeous as you do tonight. I've never seen you shine so bright. I've never seen so many people want to be there by your side, and when you turned to me and smiled, it took my breath away.[67]"

Publican: "Ahem, remember the pub rules about fraternizing – that's quite enough luffing, my friends…"

Tbc…

Comments:

YL: Dom; Every woman, once a little girl bursting with fairytales of true love and romance ultimately waits for the right guy to humbly express, "When you turned to me and smiled, it took my breath away." Thank you for reminding me.

DG: What a wonderful thought. Thank you back for reminding me, and all of us.

HG: Wonderful language! And so funny!

---

[66] "Bang, Bang", Cher, 1966
[67] "Lady in Red", Chris de Burgh, 1986

DG: Thank you - I had lots of fun with this one! Professor Nietzsche is very single-minded - oops, pardon the ambiguity - goal-oriented is a better word!

Session 4.4

Dionysus Is '86-ed' for Raving at the Pub's Anniversary Party

"I Was Only Doing My Job...Doesn't Being a God These Days Count for Anything?"

*"I'm just a soul whose intentions are good
Oh Lord - please don't let me be misunderstood."*

- *Eric Burdon & The Animals, 1977*

Dionysus: "These doings are sheer plámás[68] in search of self-aggrandization – pretentiously erudite in the extreme – practically philosophical. Everybody, even those lithe philosophers, knows that a degree of insanity is essential for happiness – let's rave!"

Publican: "Dionysus, sorry, but you are not welcome – we have more than our share of insanity present now - you are an over-prescription. By pub rule, raving should not be associated with the words stark or mad. Intuition is fine but madness goes too far. There's only so much intelligence in madness."

Friedrich Wilhelm Nietzsche: "I think you are being a bit hard on my favorite Greek God – personally, I wouldn't believe in a God that couldn't dance."

Dionysus, getting in the last word: "Dance, then, wherever you may be, I am the lord of the dance said he, and I lead you all wherever you may be, and I lead you all in the dance said he![69]"

---

[68] Wheedling flattery
[69] "Lord of the Dance", The Dubliners, 1963

Schopenhauer: "I hate parties. Dancing is much too enjoyable to be part of life. I will dance when I am safely and happily dead."

Friedrich Wilhelm Nietzsche: "Look, you've been dead for 160 years, but I've never seen you dancing!"

Erasmus of Rotterdam: "Prithee - intuition tops rationality and intelligent insanity – for theologians even more than philosophers. I've said it again and again, give a man a cape and a beard and he becomes a trouble-making philosopher. And don't even dream of giving a scientist a slide-rule."

Faust: "Can one of you Dead Viziers help me get my soul back? I was conned by the Devil who of course is the *capo di tutti capi* of conmen - I've discovered that knowing absolutely everything is not as great as it's made out to be. I'm suing in heaven's court to get my soul back in return for which I will regain my previous stupidity. But the case is taking an eternity."

...

Publican: "A toast to World Peace! To our social drinkers and our Dead Viziers, and to all of you vicarious, social-drinking world problem-solvers and commentators - long may you live!"

Dead Viziers: "Hey, gaffer, haven't you been paying attention? We're already dead and buried – being immortal and happily ensconced in heaven's bliss, we are not that interested in returning to the living."

...And the Gods danced...

Tbc...

Comments:

YL: Dom: Interesting. How many would folks already sold their souls for mere shillings (billions also qualifies)? To gain notoriety, they've consciously and defiantly broke every single commandment known to man and more. Lastly, I was amused by the possibility of being "Safely and Happily dead." There's Hope! (smile).

DG: Mellow Fellow Nietzsche's will-to-power is manifested in many ways, some of which can be nefarious...

Re the refuge of death that Schopenhauer is constantly recommending - one could also, alternatively, be "safely and happily" virtual...in the Metaverse...yes, there's Hope! (smile)

Schopenhauer: "Hey, mister, that's cheating! You shouldn't be able to leave life without dying - it's inhuman..."

HG: Wonderful dialogue! So great you got them all together!

DG: Tx!!! There's no stopping them when they get going, just like any regular session of common-or-garden social drinkers...wordy one-upmanship is rife...

Session 4.5

The Social Drinkers Ask a Serious Question:

"Are We Facing 'Darkness at Noon'*, or

'Sunshine Came Softly a-Through My a-Window Today'?**"

Schopenhauer: *"I would say that 'It's not dark yet but it's getting here.'"****

Mama Cass: *"Well, darkling Artie, I'm an optimist and everyone knows that the darkest hour is just before dawn."*****

* Arthur Koestler, 1940

** Donovan "Sunshine Superman", 1966

*** Riff on Bob Dylan, "Not Dark Yet", 1997

**** "Dedicated to the One I Love", Mamas and the Papas, 1967

Publican: "In today's digital world, each of us has a tail like a comet - we travel through digital society trailing a swirling murmuration of data. The Big Tech eagles swoop, grasp, and feed on our vast and growing murmuration. It's becoming increasingly harder to do any business or communicate without being trailed by these predators."

Head Pint: "We're being forced into a digital society - everything's on-line – banks, reservations, social interactions, metaverse, news, doctors, spas, etc.

"We're like the Eloi in The Time Machine except that it's our data that'll be eaten by terrifying monsters who don't just come out at night – they operate 24x7. We're moving towards bespoke marketing – everything you desire or even speculate about will be exactly matched by the ads you receive. They'll know our desires as well as we do ourselves.

"Eventually, many of us will be willing to pay for services that prevent this data-plundering - services which ironically will be offered by the same Big Tech corporations!"

Orwell: "Privacy is no longer possible – it is dead – I've changed my book title to '1984 + 38'. The thought police have finally arrived, and they are well-provisioned with data. Personal sovereignty is under siege.

"The Metaverse has the potential to be social media on steroids in terms of its intrusiveness and seductiveness. The data scoopers will OD on the 'big data' generated by the Metaverse.

"In addition, for life-escapees, the Metaverse's addictiveness will outpace social media's – some won't be able to resist leaving life's travails behind in the real world. Others will want to eliminate the micro-aggressions of dissenting opinions (or any opinions, for that matter) - opinions can be so disagreeable! Virtual sociability – if sociability is embraced at all - with yes-persons would be the perfect solution for them."

Head Pint: "Hold on a sec – that's very one-sided! Collaboration is the salutary aspiration offered by the promoters of the Metaverse."

Jameson 18 with a Rock: "Look, common sense tells us that competition and will-to-power of individual and special interests will be pervasive and swamp well-meaning-ness in the Metaverse as it has for much of social media today."

Pandora: "Well, social media did open my box a smidgen – I'm afraid the Metaverse could open it all the way."

Slow Pint: "So, we have privacy issues, addiction issues, self-imposed alienation, and will-to-power grappling!"

Orwell: "Plus learning is becoming a lost art – who needs to make the effort when Dr. Google and its calculators, translators, converters, and vast library can answer every question under the sun?

"Yes, we could ultimately evolve into the Eloi - technically adept but without understanding the technology, losing all knowledge of culture and reasoning, satisfied with living at ease while accomplishing little, giving up our data with a vacant smile."

Schopenhauer: "I've been saying it till I'm blue in the face - better not to have been born!"

Tbc...

HG: They put the issues so eloquently! Yes, people not knowing the basics anymore is scary! I still know my Tables up to 12×12. Do you?

DG: Ha-ha-ha! No, I just ask Google!!! Seriously, memory is a wonderful thing, even after decades and decades - amazing how the brain stashes away all the information drummed into us in primary and secondary school classes. I still remember quite a bit of Irish (Gaeilge) without having used it for over 55 years! Now, as far as short-term memory goes, that's a different matter -- now, what was I going to say?

Session 4.6

Orwell's Hobby Staves Off the Boredom of Eternal Happiness

Dionysus Swivels His Hips and Heads toward Egypt

Glum Schopenhauer Sings His Favorite Song:

"Bad is bad
I feel so sad
It's time, it's time
I found peace of mind, oh oh.

What can I do
'Cause I-I-I-I-I
I'm feelin' blue."

"Black Is Black", Los Bravos, 1966

Publican: "Phew! Is our music-led World Peace initiative just wishful thinking?"

Slow Pint: "It's not too late - the average IQ of mankind didn't increase during C-19 just because more beards were grown. We're the last bastion - our collective intuition must triumph!"

Pandora: "Sorry, but I must add one more fly to the ointment: full immersion in the Metaverse will be very expensive and complex – the populace will divide into 'haves' and 'have-nots': rich versus poor, young versus old, and software gurus versus lay-persons."

Über-bartender Ailey: "It's all quite depressing - I'd like to suggest a sure-fire, happiness-inducing, pick-me-upper: a shot of fermented blue agave juice with a squeeze of lime and a pinch of salt."

Dusty Springfield: "I'll have three of those, please. I'm just wishing and hoping and praying for us all. I am in the middle of nowhere and it's worrying me. Come show me the way."

Orwell: "Double sorry, Dusty, but there's worst <stet> news, literally - society is losing its basis in fact. All your news is spun - there's only manufactured truth."

Friedrich Wilhelm Nietzsche: "No surprise there – you've all heard me say it: there are no facts, only interpretations!"

Orwell: "Thank you - I think - Herr Professor! But yes, you're right - these days, an opinion is easily formed and promulgated via social media, but facts are hard to come by.

"Let me share a personal anecdote - contrary to popular opinion, eternal happiness in heaven can get a bit boring. I needed a hobby so - surprise, surprise - I took up an interest in propaganda and mental manipulation.

"I listen to news programs all the time. News items are now produced in the form of snappy entertainment designed to create strong emotions - cheerful or fearful. Even mostly factual weather forecasters can't escape - if it's good weather, the climate-changers point fingers; if it's bad weather, the forecasters apologize for the offence as if they were Zeus.

"Let's face it: divisiveness is good for the news and social media businesses. Convergence is losing ground to rampant divergence and trivialized irrelevancies. Remember, from peace to un-peace is a continuum – if you move away from one, you're moving nearer to the other."

Britvic Tomato Juice: "I absolutely hate where this is going. Talking about boring, may I have a splash of vodka to spruce up this over-salted, lifeless drink?

"So, you're all saying that the world is slowly rejecting its factual moorings?"

Double Red Bull: "I enjoy being factually unmoored!"

Dionysus: "Look, conventional beliefs aren't as great as they're cracked up to be...one needs to let oneself go every so often...let's twist again, like we did last summer, let's twist again, like we did last year...[70]"

Friedrich W. Nietzsche: "Where've you been for the last 60 years?"

Dionysus: "Sorry, wrong era - right-ho, let's walk like an Egyptian![71]"

<Groans>

Tbc...

Session 4.7

Are Experts No Better Than Marble Statues?

"Nothing old, nothing new, nothing ventured,
Nothing gained, nothing stillborn or lost...
Nothing physically recklessly, hopelessly blind...
'Cos today
Nothing rhymed."

- *"Nothing Rhymed", Gilbert O'Sullivan, 1971*

Mahler: "Look, didn't we agree that World Peace isn't about disarmament or defensive weapons or a MAD-induced détente?

"Peace is about music. That's our collective, firmly held belief. We need to ring the bells that still can ring, forget our perfect offering, because there's a crack in everything, and that's how the light gets in. [1]"

Visiting Mayoan [2]: "May I stick my oar in? First, thanks for inviting me. Music isn't just about peace. It's about 'anything is possible'. It can create a collective confidence and resolve – a feeling that together, we can do anything. We've demonstrated this in Mayo with our Symphony to 'The One' [3]".

---

[70] "Let's Twist Again", Chubby Checker, 1961
[71] "Walk Like and Egyptian", The Bangles, 1986

Publican: "So, not only can we use music to enable World Peace, but we can also use it to give us the collective strength and belief to accomplish it! I'd like to hear more about that."

Mayoan: "Come visit us!"

Dead Rabbit on the Rocks: "Pshaw! This whole discussion is meaningless. We're being played, literally. Life is a software program that the Gods created for their amusement - we're giving them a good laugh!"

Polymath Hypathia of Alexandria: "It's clear to me that Geraghty's social drinkers are far smarter than today's so-called experts. Combining their collective intuition with the inspiration of Mayo's Symphony to 'The One' will make us indomitable!"

Hemingway Old-Fashioned, Stiff: "The so-called experts are no better than marble statues elevated by peers to advance their own perceived importance - a mutual admiration society."

Aristotle: "I've been hearing a lot about intelligence from you people. Natural Intelligence, or NI, isn't standing still while AI improves – the purported arrival of 'The Singularity' in 2045 assumes human stasis. But human minds are also evolving.

"Moreover, sheer processing capacity isn't the best measure of the brain's capability. Electronically enhanced trans-humans are simply humans trying to be Gods - what do you bet they'll be seeking immortality next!"

Publican: "Thanks, Ari, but enough tangential levities - we need to get on with it now. After we solve World Peace with music, we'll tackle The Human of the Future, Personal Privacy, The Deformation of Society, the Meaning of Life, and Climate Change. We've a lot on our plate, so we need to give ourselves a lash!

"However, let's face it: World Peace is an existential need - if we lose peace, the rest of the problems don't matter.

"To those of you that still worry about climate change being last in the queue, don't worry. Our new friends, the Mayoans, have invented a unique renewable resource: energy derived from rainfall. Ireland is ecstatic – rain has been designated a National Treasure and Ireland has extended its Exclusive Economic Zone vertically into the clouds!

"We'll be visiting the west of Ireland to learn more about Mayo's Symphony to 'The One' and to tour its rain energy conversion project."

[1] "Anthem", Leonard Cohen, 1992
[2] Person from County Mayo, Ireland
[3] "Sumerian Vortex - Mayo Goes Mental", 2021

Session 4.8

A Paean to the Ukrainians

as

World Peace Suffers a Major Setback:

Requiescant in Pace

It's not often that words fail social drinkers but...for once, the pub is quiet - sober social drinkers talk in hushed tones, watching the flickering TV screen light up sporadically with white and yellow flashes.

There is a sense of collective shame for the world - did we all really elect these feckless politicians who are standing by with folded arms?

Publican: "There can be no laughter today - now is not a time for trivial witticisms, drollness, or clever words.

"It's a time of contemplation - anger and grim resolve will come later. Our quest for World Peace has suffered a major setback.

"Is there anything positive that can be said?

"I've asked our Dead Vizier Pericles to remind us of a comparable time in Ancient Athens when he raised the spirits and pride of assembled citizens mourning those who had lost their lives in the city-state's defense."

Pericles: "I find that I have no need to change any of the words I used 2,453 years ago[72]:

'So died these men as became patriots.

'You who remain must determine to have as unfaltering a resolution in the field, though you may pray that it may have a happier issue.

'And not contented with ideas derived only from words of the advantages which are bound up with the defense of your country, though these would furnish a valuable text to a speaker even before an audience so alive to them as the present, you must yourselves realize the power of your nation, and feed your eyes upon her from day to day, till love of her fills your hearts.

'And then, when all her greatness shall break upon you, you must reflect that it was by courage, sense of duty, and a keen feeling of honor in action that men were enabled to win all this, and that no personal failure in an enterprise could make them consent to deprive their country of their valor, but they laid it at her feet as the most glorious contribution that they could offer.

'For this offering of their lives made in common by them all, they each individually received that renown which never grows old, and for a sepulcher, not so much that in which their bones have been deposited, but that noblest of shrines wherein their glory is laid up to be eternally remembered upon every occasion on which deed or story shall call for its commemoration.

'For heroes have the whole earth for their tomb; and in lands far from their own, where the column with its epitaph declares it, there is enshrined in every breast a record unwritten with no tablet to preserve it, except that of the heart. These take as our model and, judging happiness to be the fruit of freedom and freedom of valor, never decline the dangers of war...

---

[72] Thucydides (c.460/455 - c.399 BCE): "The History of the Peloponnesian War", Book 2.34-46

'For it is only the love of honor that never grows old; and honor it is, not gain, as some would have it, that rejoices the heart of age and helplessness.'"

Silencium...

Comments:

Flaming Cosmo: "I'm laden with sadness that everyone's heart isn't filled with the gladness of love for one another. It's a long, long road from which there is no return. While we're on the way to there, why not share? [2]"

[2] "He's My Brother", The Hollies, 1969

Slow Pint: "The Eastern world, it is explodin', violence flarin', bullets loadin'...Don't you understand what I'm trying to say? Can't you feel the fear that I'm feeling today? Human respect is disintegratin', this whole crazy world is just too frustratin'. And you tell me over and over and over again, my friend, ah, you don't believe we're on the eve of destruction? [1]"

[1] "Eve of Destruction", Barry McGuire, 1965

Topic #5:

Evolution of Music: Survival

Session 5.1

The Music-Lover, the Naturalist, and the Neuroscientist:

Music on the Brain

"I can't listen to music too often. It affects your nerves, makes you want to say stupid, nice things, and stroke the heads of people who could create such beauty while living in this vile hell."

- *Vladimir Lenin, 1870-1924*

Publican: "We've all tentatively agreed that music is the answer to world peace. Now we must prove it. First, we'll talk about how music evolved; then, how it created emotions; based on this work, we'll demonstrate how we'll harness music to create world peace. It's time to move past intuition and assemble the evidence."

Slow Pint, querulously: "Evidence? I thought the use of actual evidence was banned in the pub?"

Neuroscientist: "Only written evidence is banned. Now, did y'ever wonder how we can recognize a song from the first chord? For example, the first chord of 'Hotel California' is immediately recognizable.

"The ear is a highly sound-sensitive instrument - it distinguishes the exact frequency spectrum of a musical note. It immediately recognizes individual singing voices. There are some scientists who claim that everyone is born with perfect pitch, but most lose the facility due to disuse."

Ti Punch, tinkling ice: "Word! I can easily recognize the voices of Harry Belafonte, Bob Marley, Tiny Tim, Judith Durham, Sting, Doris Day, and, of course, Leonard Cohen from the first note they sing but I couldn't tell you the key they're singing in."

Publican: "Well, good for you…Now, why do we have a visceral response to music?"

Neuroscientist: "It's a long story that started well over 100,000 years ago.

"It's been shown from fossilized remains that early humans had acute hearing and larynxes that were physiologically capable of uttering contrasting vowel sounds. The ancients had better hearing than we have today in the frequency range where vowels are articulated: 1 kHz to 3 kHz."

Flaming Cosmo: "Vowel sounds? Just like when Slow Pint coos sweet nothings to me!"

Slow Pint: "I'm a cooing wooer, amn't I?"

Neuroscientist: "Ahem…Modern man developed improved hearing in the 1 kHz - 6 kHz because it was necessary for recognizing pronounced consonants in speech. So, our genes have been hard at work.

"As ancient humans listened to animals, they discovered that they could reproduce these vowel-like sounds themselves.

"The brain carefully stored the sounds and developed a mechanism to instantly recall them.

"As time went on, early humans discovered that they could increase their chances of survival if they formed cooperative groups. To communicate, it is likely that humans articulated the sounds they knew, accompanied by gestures. This communication developed into musi-language. Charles, I see you'd like to add something?"

Charles R. Darwin, FRS, FRGS, FLS, FZS: "I've thought about this a lot. When you're becalmed on the high seas for weeks, there isn't much else to do. Musi-language came before proto-language. Communication evolved from tonal grunts and gestures to meaningful sounds and body movements.

"The different tones conveyed different emotions. A form of primitive tonal music became the lingua franca."

Glass of Stout: "My wife uses proto-language sometimes - I'm not always sure what she means but I can definitely feel the emotions!"

Tbc...

Comments:

YL: Dom: I can't believe "Ti Punch" mentioned, "Tiny Tim." OMG! 😄 If memory serves me correctly, he was a frequent guest on "The Ed Sullivan Show." In addition, I really like "Sting," because he's very organic, spirited, and unpretentious. Moreover, I believe his hit song entitled, "Free, Free, Set Them Free" could be a serious contender.

DG: Yes, Yo - Tiny Tim sang "Tiptoe Through the Tulips" in falsetto, accompanied himself with his ukulele!

Sting - now that's a voice you can recognize from the first moment he starts singing! My favorite is "Fields of Green".

His hit love-song - "If You Love Somebody, Set Them Free" is very recognizable and triggers experiential memory endorphins for those who grew up with it.

Hint of things to come: in their quest to find music that creates World Peace, the Social Drinkers and their friend the neuroscientist will discuss in the near future how/why experiential music creates anticipative emotions that release puffs of dopamine in the brain and sometimes even create goosebumps. Perhaps they can corral that effect and incorporate it into their World Peace symphony - who knows?

Session 5.2

Music: Early Humans' Survival, Ritual, and Mate-Finding

"You get a shiver in the dark
It's a raining in the park but meantime -
South of the river you stop, and you hold everything
A band is blowing Dixie, double four time
You feel alright when you hear the music ring."

"Sultans of Swing", Dire Straits, 1978

Darwin, without missing a beat: "Humans being social animals, the tonal musi-language expanded. In pre-historic group settings, social rituals were developed where the group intoned and moved their bodies in synchronization - like today's music and dancing at a rave to electro-music. Rhythm was a sign of life and rhythmic sound was the sound of the living.

"Rhythmic synchronization also sent a signal of social cohesion to potential predators and rival groups.

"Our human ancestors discovered that these social rituals created pleasant feelings of empathy for the others in their group. This led to trust and cooperation, and the cooperation created increased prosperity over time."

Shandyman: "Well, isn't buying rounds of drinks in Geraghty's a cooperative activity reliant on trust and empathy?"

Darwin: "Does everything for you have to revolve around social drinking? Clearly, you are not fully evolved!

"The musi-language was passed down from generation to generation. It became more sophisticated, eventually leading to the branching off of language and speech from the music itself."

Slow Pint: "So, are you saying that proto-music conveyed emotions in the same way music does today?"

Neuroscientist: "Yes. The question is how. Actually, music is a drug pusher of sorts. We know that combinations of tones create different emotions, as the good and bad tones did for primitive groups of the past. For remembered music, it is generally believed that anticipation releases pleasure hormones such as dopamine and oxytocin - hormones that give us pleasure and increase our propensity for empathy and conviviality.

"Pleasant musical surprises that stray from anticipation provide further releases of these hormones. These responses are important because empathy and conviviality are crucial elements in our quest to use music to achieve world peace."

Drink: "Some people enjoy a piece of music so much that they feel goosebumps. These are caused mainly by the release of adrenaline in the body - a physiological response by the brain to pleasure."

Neuroscientist: "Yes. However, as far as the ancient parts of our brain are concerned, music is not just a random bit of fun or an accompaniment to dancing. Music processing is engrained in our brain because it was originally critical for survival.

"For tens of thousands of years, the brain preserved music processing to preserve our species. Music is innate. It is in our genes! Even new-born infants respond to music and its rhythms.

"Hardwiring of most of the brain's network takes place before birth according to a pre-programmed genetic blueprint, without external influences taking a role. Only a relatively small number of synapses are wired by learning experiences.

"So, the brain continues to use this ancient, hard-wired mechanism through today. Music still creates social cohesion, empathy, and a range of emotions. It is this ability that we need to harness to create world peace."

Session 5.3
The Sounds of Music Are in Our Genes

"In prehistoric times, music, like dance and every other artistic endeavor, was a branch of magic, one of the old and legitimate instruments of wonder-working. Beginning with rhythm (clapping of hands, tramping, beating of sticks and primitive drums), it was a powerful, tried-and-true device for putting a large number of people "in tune" with one another, engendering the same mood, co-coordinating the pace of their breathing and heartbeats, encouraging them to invoke and conjure up the eternal powers, to dance, to compete, to make war, to worship. And music has retained this original, pure, primordially powerful character, its magic, far longer than the other arts."

- *Herman Hesse, "The Glass Bead Game/Magister Ludi", 1943*

Publican: "How does our music processing work physiologically?"

Neuroscientist: "Here's what we know. Given our ability to easily recognize a song or a singer, our music processing must be high-resolution. Music consists of fundamental frequencies (the music tone) and harmonic frequencies associated with the fundamental. The harmonics provide the distinguishing timbre of the sound - they vary in amplitude and are lower than the fundamental in loudness.

"The ear senses frequencies very accurately. It has about 3,500 frequency-sensing hairs. Each hair takes ownership of a distinct sliver of frequency and pulses it through the tuned fibers of the auditory nerve to the auditory cortex.

"The ear's frequency range is 20 Hz to 20 kHz - the frequency spectrum of music is somewhat narrower than that. Musical instruments have a wide variety of frequency ranges (from 35 Hz to 5,000 Hz). Each instrument produces a unique harmonic spectrum. This variety results in a practically infinite number of permutations of musical patterns.

"Yes, a tone is really a pattern of harmonics; music is a series of these patterns. Since harmonics contain a lot of information – frequencies, intensity, and rhythm, a huge amount of brain storage is required. Yet a stored pattern is accessible in milliseconds - the brain's retrieval ability is astonishing. You hear 20 to 100 times faster than you see. Sound is very direct."

Slow Pint: "You already told us that the frequency range of conversational speech is in the frequency range 125Hz to 8,000 Hz. What is the frequency range of music?"

Neuroscientist: "A human's singing voice frequency range is 75 Hz - 1,200Hz."

Slow Pint: "I've another question: why are we not able to hear high pitches? Some mammals have much better hearing than we humans. For example, bats can hear up to 200 kHz."

Neuroscientist: "Are you planning to fly round in the dark with your eyes closed? No, I didn't think so. The answer is simple. Our genes must have decided that high-frequency echolocation wasn't necessary for our survival.

"The brain is a very efficient organ. It can even cancel sounds that it deems irrelevant - for example, a lawnmower, overhead jet, leaf blower, or a train-whistle. You don't notice them anymore unless you are actively listening. It's like the brain is saying: 'I recognize that sound - it is in my memory. It is not important to this body physically or emotionally, so I'll ignore it.'"

Glass of Stout: "I sometimes have the opposite problem. Have you ever had music on your brain?

"Why does a certain music phrase keep repeating in my mind if it is not being summoned by the brain? It drives me crazy!"

Neuroscientist: "'Earworms' are quite common. You are not - ahem - batty. It's a mystery why we 'hear' unwilled music in our brain. Wilhelm Richard, you seem to be getting restless?"

Topic #6:

Jackdaw and Magpie

Session 6.1

Meet the Enigmatic Jackdaw and Magpie - Strangers in the Night

Watch Cosmo Flaming Out as She Moves in Mysterious Ways

"Saol na saol (Life of lives)

Tús go deireadh (Start to end)

Tá muid beo (We are alive)

Go deo." (Forever)

- "The Celts", Enya, 1987

That evening, two strangers - a man and woman - had shown up at Geraghty's. They sat quietly listening to the social drinkers bemoaning societal divergence and debating about how to reverse this trend toward world peace.

The couple ordered their drinks: two Lady Janes, Cucumber Slices, in beakers.

Ailey, Über-bartender: "Ah, this will take me a while - it won't be coming right up! I'll start the fermentation now - luckily, I purchased a fermentation accelerator last month to accommodate drinkers with a Celtic bent."

Head Pint to the couple: "Welcome to Geraghty's, strangers! If I may take the liberty: what brings you to these hallowed grounds?"

The man introduced himself: "I am Jack Dawulff von der Graf – you can call me Jackdaw. This is my S.O.: Magyar Pye from Budapest."

S.O.: "Please don't call me Maggie, call me Magpie."

Publican (sotto voce): "Hmmm...so it's Jackdaw and Magpie. If they don't sound like *noms de plume*, I don't know what does."

Head Pint to Jackdaw: "I detect a slight accent. Where might you hail from?"

Jackdaw sipping his bog-heather mead - a surprisingly good concoction by Ailey: "Oh, here and there", he said airily. "I am a direct descendent of the Hallstatt Celts of middle Europe. You may remember that they originated in Upper Austria in 800 B.C. and went on to conquer large swaths of Europe.

"We've been following the paths of these ancient Celts across Europe. Recently, we were in Ireland - County Mayo to be exact. I have a twin brother there who is doing some research in the area where the Hallstatt Celts first landed. After spending a few intensive months there, we decided that it was time for us to take a break.

"We heard about your social drinkers' productive shenanigans - ahem - problem-solving, which, as I'm sure you all know, mirrors the methodology that the Celts used for their momentous invasion decisions as they conquered the length and breadth of Europe. So, you are present-day druids - I'll wager you have a lot of Celtic genes in your midst!"

At the other end of the pub, Geraghty's visitor from Mayo was nonplussed. He had never heard of those two strangers - never mind meeting them. He was amazed when Jackdaw mentioned that he had a twin brother living in Mayo, thinking: 'I knew about our resident Austrian, Gernot, and his twin brother - I had no idea that they were triplets!'

Flaming Cosmo, intrigued by the mysterious, well-traveled stranger with the exotic accent, shook her red hair alluringly: "Tell us much more! Pardon the way that I stare, there's nothing else to compare. The sight of you leaves me weak. There are no words left to speak.[73]"

Slow Pint: "You are in a no-fly zone, Ms. Cosmo - a little bird told me that Jackdaw and Magpie are birds of a feather. Look, he's just a fly-by-

---

[73] "Can't Take My Eyes Off You", Frankie Valli and the 4 Seasons, 1967

night - there's no need to feather his nest. My butterfly, wait for me - don't fly away.[74]"

Tbc...

Session 6.2

Jackdaw and Magpie Talk About Fakers, Breakers, Shakers, and Quakers

"We've lost that lovin' feelin'
Whoa, that lovin' feelin'
We've lost that lovin' feelin'
Now it's gone, gone, gone, whoa-oh...

And we can't go on, whoa-oh."

- *"You've Lost That Lovin' Feelin'", The Righteous Brothers, 1965*

Jackdaw, smiling: "Time enough for that, my dear lady in red. Let's chat later. Right now, I have a more pertinent matter to broach.

"I'm told that in this pub every opinion will be listened to. Well, this is my opinion: your pursuit of World Peace, worthy though it may be, is futile - you're all wasting your sweetness on the desert air. You can make no difference because world society is so obviously headed for dystopia. There's nothing you can do about it.

"In fact, there's not a moment to lose - if you want to live by your own standards, you must create your own place.

"I really like your idea of using music to create world peace, but you've too many powerful entities against you. You've the powerful elites, the wealthy, and the bankers who do not want World Peace - it is bad for business and dents their accumulation of power.

---

[74] "Butterfly", Jim Ed Brown, 1972

"You've the fakers, breakers, shakers, and quakers; the haters, looters, victors and victims, and be-grudgers; the plutocratic dividers: politicians, divas, celebrities, aristocracy, gentry, and patricians; the Deep State, policy wonks, academia, and experts who are comfortably nested in their sinecures.

"Last but not least, you're dealing with the resurrection of modern-day Thought Police. Yes, a phalanx of forces is lined up against you."

Magpie, taking up the harangue: "What you're attempting to achieve is impossible! And forget about expanding your Metaverse. I say confine its use solely to facilitate the collaboration of your far-flung social drinkers in your problem-solving programs.

"You need to escape to an alternative reality, not unreality! You can offer up your best defense, but this is the end, this is the end of the innocence[75]."

Jackdaw: "Look, hardly any peace-softened body is willing to sacrifice its relatively low-risk, good life to fight for societal convergence - except you and the Ukrainians, perhaps. Nobody wants to rock the boat - these ostriches have their heads in the sand!"

Samuel Beckett: "Any fool can turn a blind eye, but who knows what the ostrich sees in the sand? And take it from me - don't wait for divine intervention - Godot never comes."

Publican: "Well, Jackdaw and Maggie - your views are very dark. We do not agree that peace is impossible, but there's no doubt that society is diverging.

"I began to worry when the Canadian truckers organized a protest opposing their government's fiats. The most amiable people in the world live in Canada and yet the government vilified its truckers, suppressed their freedom of speech, and froze their bank accounts - totalitarianism in full view.

[75] "The End of the Innocence", Don Henley, 1989

"Then there was Australia - another traditionally-easy-going country where citizens experienced interminable, draconian clampdowns on any movement during Covid - assiduously enforced with no-second-chance arrests by the police.

"And we have the continuing factional polarization in the EU, UK, and USA.

"So, yes, signs are we are up against it and need a Plan B."

Comments:

YL: To be on the safe side, they should also consider developing a Plan C as well. ☺

DG: That is so funny!!! I don't think you are taking me seriously enough!!! ☺

YL: Of course, I am. Keep in mind, a key person could drop dead in the middle of the night or suffer amnesia. You get the picture (smile).

DG: Now, Yo, those are scary thoughts...Luckily, Geraghty's already has a neurologist on staff to monitor the level of insanity amongst the social drinkers - I will ask her to look out for amnesia attacks - while calibrating of course for the number of pints imbibed. The Publican wants me to thank you for reminding him that he needs to work on his succession plan (Plan C) and get some more exercise (beyond his daily reps lifting full pint glasses) - he does not want to meet a bucket he has to kick anytime soon... ☺

Session 6.3

Are Jackdaw and Magpie Fly-By-Nights?

Is Mayo Nation Too Good to Be True?

The Infamous Rhizommelier Makes a Flying Visit

"Time goes by on the parallel
On the streets of fire
Burning songs from a dark hallway
Echo now through the never, never, never
And your life becomes just a ritual...

We run to catch the moon
We dance under the sun
We run to catch the moon."

- *"Catch the Moon", Marc Jordan, 1987*

Magpie piled on: "I say: flip World Peace - it's horse-apples - an impossible dream!"

Flaming Cosmo: "Well, I don't want to dream the impossible dream or fight the unbeatable foe. This is not my quest. Why should I follow that star, ooh, no matter how hopeless, no matter how far? Why should I be willing to go into hell for an un-heavenly cause?[76]"

Magpie: "That's more like it - now you're getting a grip! You need to save your own way of living."

Jackdaw: "Look, I have a suggestion about a very peaceful, harmonious, self-sufficient, musical place that can offer a compatible haven for you: Mayo Nation - a new nation that achieved independence from the Irish republic in 2021[77]. I have many friends there and, and, as you know, some family too."

---

[76] "The Impossible Dream", Luther Vandross, 1994 (adapted)
[77] "Sumerian Vortex - Mayo Goes Mental", 2021

Rhizommelier[78], suddenly appearing: "I thought mayo was used as a condiment for pommes frites?"

Jackdaw: "Ah, talking about hot potatoes, it's none other than Chef Niamh's M. Rhizommelier! I've heard about your odd obsession with potatoes. Don't you have a court injunction to stay at least 100 meters from defenseless tubers?"

Rhizommelier[79]: "Qu'est-ce que c'est que ça? I have moved on to orchids since that ugly contretemps - they are much more soothing. Mais je manque beaucoup mes amis - les beaux pommes de terre au buerre - très savoureaux!"

Publican, smacking his lips, flustered: "Mmmm…never mind! Now, where was I? Ah, yes - Jackdaw, why do you think that Geraghty's and Mayo Nation are compatible entities?"

Jackdaw described Mayo's constitution, governance, and Grand Plan[80]. The latter had achieved an impressive list of accomplishments benefiting Mayoans. It seemed a far cry from the toxic politics, political correctness, and unrepresentative representatives of the social drinkers' milieu. They and the Dead Viziers could find little to quibble about, at least not on the surface.

But was Jackdaw just a great spin-doctor? Was Magpie a Siren singing them onto a rocky shore?

One way or another, they'd need to find out, but it was certainly worth a look.

Faust: "Mayo sounds like heaven on earth! I would love to move there - it is hell where I am."

---

[78] "Confessions of a Pop-Pampering Rhizommelier", Episode #18, LinkedIn Post, 5/3/21 and "The Dreaded Rhizommelier Is Back". Episode #25, LinkedIn Post, 6/14/21
[79] "Confessions of a Pop-Pampering Rhizommelier", Post #18, LinkedIn, 5/3/21
[80] "Sumerian Vortex - Music from a Lost Civilization", 2020, and "Sumerian Vortex - Mayo Goes Mental", 2021

Erasmus: "I've been in heaven for eons and pure happiness is getting a bit boring. You are right, Johann, Mayo sounds like heaven on earth, but with some intriguing, unpredictable free-will foibles. I wouldn't mind teetering around a happiness median for a change."

Schopenhauer: "Pshaw! Mayo is too good to be true. I can't believe that there is anywhere on earth where one can be happy."

Tbc...

Session 6.4

Jackdaw and Magpie Invite Geraghty's to Visit Mayo Nation:

"No Need to Bring Your Waterproofs or Brollies!"

"Is the struggle and strife we find in this life
Really worthwhile, after all
I've been wishing today I could just run away
Out where the west winds call...

We'll find perfect peace, where joys never cease
Out there beneath a kindly sky
We'll build a sweet little nest somewhere in the west
And let the rest of the world go by."

"Let the Rest of the World Go By", Albert Campbell and Henry Burr, 1919

Slow Pint: "Now, hold on with all this nirvana stuff - isn't Mayo very rainy, with incessant Atlantic storms of salty winds? Don't Mayoans have 23 different words for rain? What's the suicide rate like?"

Jackdaw: "Funny you should mention weather - Mayoans have developed a micro-climate management system that extracts energy from raindrops that keep falling on their heads, while simultaneously decreasing cloud cover. The nation now has some balmy, low-humidity,

Mayoterranean micro-climates - wineries and date palms are common sights. Skin cancer is on the rise for those fair-skinned Celts."

Magpie: "I say let the rest of the world go its way, and you go yours. We can introduce you to Mayo's leadership team. You have a lot in common and there are synergies between your use of music for peace and Mayo's use of music to create limitless confidence in human potential.

"In order to prolong the empathetic effect of its Harmony Day music, Mayo is also interested in the interaction between the brain and music, something that Geraghty's' social drinkers have been working on for quite a while. It seems to me that your 'Peace Rhapsody' and Mayo's 'Harmony Day' music are one of a piece. Collaboration on perfecting a joint music composition could be a win-win endeavor."

Publican (thinking): 'Jackdaw and Magpie seem very pushy - I wonder what's in it for them. I sense the coming of a quid pro quo.'

Jackdaw, as if he had read the Publican's thoughts: "Look, we don't want to force the issue - do some due diligence in Mayo and then decide -- we'd be happy to show you around."

Mayo Visitor, emerging from the back of the pub: "You know, a collaboration between Mayo and Geraghty's might work. Mayo is aware that it can never be self-sufficient in intellectual horsepower - it could use the collective intuition belching out from your social drinkers."

Publican: "Well, we are not ready to give up on Plan A yet, but we'll visit Mayo and as you suggest, meet the leadership, and conduct some due diligence.

"However, we are very busy right now working on the design of our World Peace musical composition while reining in some apostates in our midst - including some Dead Viziers who aren't fully on board.

"Can we set a date for a visit about two months hence?"

Jackdaw: "I'll check with the leadership in Mayo, but I think that will be fine...I'm very glad we dropped in on Geraghty's tonight!"

Magpie to Ailey: "By the way, I love your bracelet - it's so shiny!"

Tbc...

Dominic Geraghty

Topic #7:

Meet Chief Neuronimo

Session 7.1

The Magic of Music

"Remember when the days were long
And rolled beneath a deep blue sky
Didn't have a care in the world
With mommy and daddy standing by
When "happily ever after" fails
And we've been poisoned by these fairy tales
The lawyers dwell on small details
Since daddy had to fly."

"The End of the Innocence", Don Henley, 1989

Maestro Herr W. R. Wagner: "This is all very <yawn> interesting and we're certainly on the right track but, don't forget, we need to connect your meanderings to world peace. Look, I've been manipulating emotions with music for over 150 years.

"When do we get to the good stuff - that is, composing our Symphony to World Peace? Let's get to the music!"

Publican: "Patience, Ricky, patience. We must understand the physics, the neuroscience, the social science, and the magic of music. We must bring all of these together in order to perfect the composition of our world peace music."

Glass of Stout: "Hold on a second! Couldn't the emotional effect of music also be subjective - influenced just as much by a person's music experiences as their genes - a kind-of resonance with a person's remembered-music?"

Neuroscientist: "Great question! Early-age exposure and our life's music experiences mediate how music triggers our emotions. Our brain doesn't forget music. When we listen to it, therefore, our music-processing neurons create expectations of the next notes we we'll hear."

Freud: "Ahem - may I stick my oar in? Music has a purpose looking from the other end of life too. Psychologically, music is a way backwards in your life to when you first heard it. We never forget fond memories - they're palliatives that sooth our fears of immortality. The pleasure of music associated with your 'lived life' can ameliorate the fear of death."

Neuroscientist: "Very interesting, Ziggy - so, that's yet one more way that music can create positive emotions. But where do the emotions come from? Let's take a classic symphony. The piece is known, the progress of the music is predictable. The brain immediately detects any deviations as it matches the music with its stored music library.

"Every maestro plays the same music differently. While the fundamental tones are the same and in the same sequence - the brain hears and anticipates the next note based on our experiences. The virtuoso creates a great concert by customizing the timbre (technically, the waveform) of the music - adding pleasant surprises which release pleasure hormones.

"In a 'flat' concert, the brain becomes bored and starts canceling the music automatically, just like when you hear the same pop song over and over - great at the start, boring later because it never changes. How many times have you seen people falling asleep in symphony halls?

Wagner: "I've been told that my operas are exhausting!"

Neuroscientist: "Plus, it's not just changes in the timbre - it's also possible for the musician, singer, or conductor to change the rhythm in a composition, something that would again be immediately perceived by the brain. Rhythm reminds the brain of the rhythm of life - to the brain, musical rhythms are proof-of-life rhythms."

Slow Pint: "Yes, the rhythm of life's a powerful feeling, puts a tingle in your fingers and a tingle in your feet.[81]"

---

[81]"Rhythm of Life", Sammy Davis Jr., in "Sweet Charity", 1969

Session 7.2

Musical Memory-Traces

Music and Goosebumps

"Now as the years roll on
Each time we hear our favorite song
The memories come along
Older times we're missing
Spending the hours reminiscing.

Hurry, don't be late, I can hardly wait
I said to myself when we're old
We'll go dancing in the dark
Walking through the park and reminiscing."

- *"Reminiscing", Little River Band, 1978*

Neuroscientist: "Accumulated musical experiences in life create expectations in the listener that trigger pleasurable emotions - musical surprises add to this emotional impact."

Shandyman: "Aren't emotional reactions to music person- and culture-specific? Does this diversity of reactions create a challenge for us in designing universal music that spans across all of mankind?"

Maestro Herr W. R. Wagner: "Excellent point, Herr Radler. Our Symphony to World Peace must bridge across personal differences and cultural lines."

Double Red Bull, twitching: "Look, enough of these conjectures and aspirations! Besides the release of feel-good drugs, what's happening in the brain? Tell me about the neuroscience!"

Neuroscientist: "Well, we don't know exactly. The way the brain processes music seems to be different to other brain processes. Once they evolve a design for survival, genes can be intransigent buggers! They've a memory like elephants if you'll pardon the mixed metaphor.

Why should the genes jettison a processing scheme that has proven its value and endured since the times of ancient man?

"There are thousands of medical examples that support the view that music processes in the brain are unique: a seriously damaged brain can still remember music, play it, sing it, while not functioning in many other ways. It seems that neuronal memory-traces built through music are deeply engrained and resilient to neurodegeneration influences."

Darwin: "The brain is telling us something very important: music is so critical to life that the brain has devised a unique way to memorize and protect it from bodily calamities. This isn't an accident."

Neuroscientist: "Here's one possible storage mechanism that the brain might employ. Sound is a wave. Waves encountering objects create diffraction patterns. Remember walking the beach and seeing the compound ripples of retreating waves around rocks?

"A similar system of diffraction is the principle used in holography. It could be that the brain reconstructs music memories just like a laser reconstructs a hologram, integrating all the diffracted phases of the sound waves – remember, the brain is a consummate pattern-recognition machine.

"Holograms are a highly efficient way to store a lot of information securely - even if one part of the storage is lost, the music can still be reconstructed from the remaining phase patterns. That is, each part of the hologram contains all the information of the original interference patterns, albeit at lower resolution.

"That could explain why music memory survives in damaged brains - the pattern can always be reconstructed even when some of the data is lost."

Einstein: "There's another question: how does the brain recognize heard music? Surely it doesn't search its entire distributed music memory - that'd be very inefficient and time consuming and it wouldn't conform to the fast-response evidence we observe. There's only one way it can happen: resonance!

Comments:

YL: Dom ☺; Last week, for some odd reason, I began lightly singing the noted "Little River Band" song. 'Walking through the park and reminiscing...' It's an inspiring song. Words to live by. Thank you for reminding me.

DG: What a coincidence! Yes, Yo, wonderful melodies, and words like that remind us of where we were in 1978 and resuscitate memories that have been stashed indelibly in our brains alongside the music - I guess that's what reminiscing is about!

Session 7.3

Buskers Create Peace a Few Persons at a Time

"I listened, motionless and still;
And, as I mounted up the hill,
The music in my heart I bore,
Long after it was heard no more."

- *"The Solitary Reaper", William Wordsworth, 1770-1850*

Einstein, continuing: "Resonance-seeking eliminates the need to search through all harmonic patterns in the brain. It allows for a rapidly converging search for a resonant harmonic memory of the music being heard.

"Think of an airplane starting up its second jet engine and the resonating 'beats' as it closes in on the sound frequency of the other jet engine.

"If the brain senses a resonance connected to a memory - bingo - the music is recognized."

Hypathia, polymath of Alexandria: "My dear living and dead people, we've given ourselves a lot to think about. Let me summarize where we are.

"Music has accompanied human civilization since time immemorial. It affected social behavior positively and it still does. We are not exactly sure why.

Comments:

YL: Dom ☺; I'm curious what will be chosen as the "Final Masterpiece." There are so many great songs to choose from. Perhaps, the group will decide to select one special from 1950-Present. Good Luck!

DG: Actually, all those memorable, beautiful songs of the past century are inadequate, great though they are. Even "Imagine" is not enough. It will not be a 3 - 6 minutes song...the social drinkers are thinking more of a Rhapsody or Symphony to Peace.

The music will need to sync with the physiology of the body and the rhythms of the brain and cancel those so that minds and souls are free to soar far above their earthly bodies to join with other souls in limitless empathy and confidence in the unity of all souls - "The One".

How is that going to be done? Well, we will meet Chief Neuronimo in the next post and he will clear up some, but not all, things.

Comments:

YL: Dom ☺; Let's hope that he'll @ least give us a decent clue. Either that, or breadcrumbs (lol).

DG: Hint: Everything is Vibration.

YL: Dom; Geez! ☺ Could you also inquire whether we'll need any stereo equipment in particular? Thanks!

DG: You can rely on Chief Neuronimo - if he can handle billions and billions of neurons and synapses, what would a simple Symphony to Peace be to him? No need for extra stereo or surround-sound equipment - just bring your mind - the social drinkers are responsible for reaching your ears, and your ears for reaching your mind.

YL: Dom☺; Sounds Heavenly. Hopefully, we'll be alive to enjoy the Meta experience!

DG: Don't worry, one way or another, Geraghty's social drinkers will find a solution while we are still alive!

JR: There is a peace in the pathless woods
There is a rapture by the lonely shore
There is society where none intrudes
By the deep sea, and music in its roar
I love not man the less, but nature more.

Session 7.4

Meet Chief Neuronimo and His Army of 120 Billion Neurons and Quadrillion Synapses (Part 1)

"What would you think if I sang out of tune?
Would you stand up and walk out on me?
Lend me your ears and I'll sing you a song
And I'll try not to sing out of key
Oh, I get by with a little help from my friends."

- *The Beatles, 1967*

It was a dark and stormy night. Grim social drinkers sat hunched around small tables in Geraghty's, pints untouched – silencium! Flickering Zoom screens brightened the gloom, displaying countless images of virtual drinkers assembled for the session. They had run out of speculations - they needed some actual facts to continue.

Publican: "We've hypothesized about the human brain's mechanism for processing music. Now we need a scientific basis to corroborate our theories.

"I'm delighted to announce that Asclepius, the God of Medicine and son of Apollo, has graciously invited a surprise guest to help us understand the inner workings of the brain."

Pale Ale, brightening: "I've never heard of Asclepius, but with a God on our side, how can we fail?"

A fuzzy image of a dense network materialized on the Zoom screens - it metamorphosed into a human skull, festooned with frondish dendrites.

"Hello, I am Chief Neuronimo, leader of the Neurons on Axonax - that's what we neurons call our human brain. Nice to meet you all.

"I'm very, very busy. I've a 24x7 job. I never sleep, but I can spare 15 minutes to tell you about my operation. However, no interruptions, please - they upset my patterns."

Slow Pint: "15 minutes? That's about a half-a-pint on the Social Drinking Imbibement Timescale, assuming a non-turbulent Reynolds number."

Chief Neuronimo: "Where to begin? I preside over a huge network run by a vast army.

"My nerve fiber network is 500,000 kilometers long - it's a massive communications and delivery network of main roads, secondary roads, byways, lanes, and paths. The crossroads shift continuously.

"My synchronized marching band of 100 billion neurons feed one quadrillion synapses. To get a feel for that number, think of the U.S. national debt by 2050. Essentially, I am the drum major of these centibillion neurons deployed in cohorts across the vast territories of the brain.

"Each of my neurons is connected to up to 10,000 fellow-neurons, passing signals to each other via synaptic connections. The amount of traffic is stupendous - it's busier than Shinjuku station at rush hour."

Coco Loco: "I don't think you've ever been to Bogota, have you?"

Chief N.: "I have regional offices all over the brain from the frontal cortex to the spinal cord. Since messages often concern life or death matters, a traffic jam would be catastrophic. My network must be robust, redundant, and resilient.

"I am the traffic policeman for the entire shebang. Think of it - I manage 1,000 trillion intersections!

"My neurons create ever-changing and very precise patterns of connections in milliseconds - they look like a murmuration of flying starlings, but they move infinitely faster. They pulsate in waves, sweeping and swirling into an array of patterns at speeds faster than high-frequency traders."

Tbc...

YL: Dom☺; I've just figured out why I like your style of writing. Besides the language being exceptional and unique, it reminds me of a 60's Sci-Fi movie. If I was well-connected, I would contact our flagship leader ("Bezos"- since we're both published under his label), and ask, "How about making an out-of-this world 📽? " ☺

DG: Yo, thank you! Yes, I go to pains to be technically correct and to weave technology into the story (sometimes to the detriment of my grip on the reader). I am a closet (?) technophile.

Related to your idea of a Bezotic movie, I have been encouraged by several critics to explore a TV series because the chapters in my books tend to be stand-alone episodes of the story.

But underneath the antics, fantasy, and allegory of my writings, I am deadly serious - as you shall see when my upcoming book finally emerges from the roiling waters of pre-pub franticness. D.

Dom☺; Keep going! Needless to say, I'm a fan of your hard work.

JI: You are WAY out of the closet as a technophile. More like the Barnum Bailey of technophiles, but no neurons are harmed in the production. Enjoying your stories.

DG: Hi Jeff, you remind me of Zola: "J'Accuse!" And I cannot in all consciousness plead anything but guilty as charged. Delighted that u r enjoying my ruminations...

Or as they said in Chicago in the 1890s: "Jackuse!" (Finley Peter Dunne)

DG: Tx, Yo, I shall soldier on unburdening myself on blameless and unsuspecting readers!

CC: Dominic, we probably need more Ni-Ki-Yyr technologies these days...

DG: Hi Christian! Yes, your frequency management expertise shines through!!! I think that the harmonic music of the Ni-Ki-Yyr (1) would do all of us a world of good! Pythagoras said that: "All is number", but Einstein said: "All is vibration (frequency)", and I think Albert had it right.

Namaste...

(1) For those who have not heard about the mysterious Ni-Ki-Yyr: it is an ancient Sumerian frequency management system that broadcast euphoria-inducing music in the Sumerian Vortex book series...

Session 7.5

Meet Chief Neuronimo, Head of an Army of 20 Billion Neurons and a Quadrillion Synapses (Part 2)

Chief Neuronimo: "Let's start with a single neuron or nerve cell - I'm putting a diagram on your Zoom screen right now (see inset). This is just one of over 100 billion nerve cells in our brains. A nerve cell has multiple channels called dendrites - they look like fern fronds. Dendrites are one-way receptors that bring information into the neuron through many pathways.

"A neuron's output channel is just a single axon or nerve fiber. It is a high-capacity transmission cable - a wide freeway - ranging in length from 1 mm to 1 meter. Axons that are far away from brain H.Q. are like missionaries - they can sometimes be hard to control, but their hearts are in the right place.

"Running the brain is very stressful for our Human Resources Dept. - demands, demands, demands - never a dull moment. Not alone am I a traffic cop, but I have to manage the neuron career path.

"Every neuron wants to be in the brain's music center because it connects with so many other brain regions - you meet lots of interesting synapses and travel along miles of axons through all sorts of scenic biology."

Glass of Cab: "I'm pretty sure that blood vessels and brain matter would not be my definition of uplifting scenery."

Chief Neuronimo: "Unfunny. We have a flat organization - promotions are few and far between. Besides, when you are trained for a specialized cranial function, retraining is time-consuming, and we just don't have the budget or neuron-power."

Publican: "That's all very impressive and you are obviously doing an admirable job under very stringent conditions. However, we are interested in how you process music because we want to use music to achieve world peace."

Chief Neuronimo: "Patience - I'm getting there. The brainpower of your social drinkers is quite extraordinary, I must say - and I know all there is to know about brains. Your brain trust is on the mark.

"You ask how we process music in the brain. <Sigh>

"Let me talk first about our dark secret because it pertains to music: we are dealing with an epidemic of drug-dealing on Axonax. Music is not just about the pleasures of traveling along axons and around my network.

"My neurons have a problem with addiction to the pleasure drugs: oxytocin, dopamine, and noradrenaline. Neurons work 24x7. Drugs are their escape - they love to zone out on oxytocin especially.

"After seeing music neurons getting high on my pleasure drugs, my common-or-garden neurons wanted some themselves. I tried to point out that the music neurons needed these neurotransmitters to - ahem - conduct their work, but, no, my pesky peon-neurons wouldn't listen - they wanted in on the drug traffic."

Sparkling Water: "Why don't you send them out for a jog along those kilometers of pathways in your demesne? It'd be very healthy and would offer the prospect of a nice puff or two of dopamine."

Chief Neuronimo: "As if! Instead of doing their jobs, I have mobs of neurons roaming around looking for drugs. Brain productivity has plummeted."

Tbc...

Comments:

YL: Dom 😊 ; Briefly, I just gain an opportunity to tune in. Of course, I found all the characters quite interesting, especially the traffic cop; the drug epidemic, and just when you believe that you've heard it all, Chief Neuronimo cries about lacking a sufficient budget. Sounds like City Hall and Old Sac to me!

DG: City Hall and Old Sac!!! Ha-ha-ha...

However, the brain is not a classical liberal democracy! Chief Neuronimo must perforce be an autocrat. There is no room for 'do-nothing' neurocrats - decision-making must be swift and decisive, given that it often involves life-or-death situations.

So, lower-level peon-neurons are worked to the bone while elite music neurons laze on sunny afternoons.

Right underneath the surface, there is unrest in Axonax. There are rumors that the peon-neurons are going out on strike - they want their 'fair share' of dopamine and oxytocin. They maintain that the music neurons are monopolizing the brain's limited supply of pleasure drugs while the peon-neurons are doing most of the work to place and relocate musical resonances in memory:

"Sorry, Chief, but your administration is treating us like slaves without even a single indenture. We demand equal opportunity drugs, or we'll close down your axons and dendrites, create tinnitus - see how the music neurons will enjoy that! Plus, we'll stop reproducing to boot."

You can imagine where this hare-brained threat might lead...

YL: Dom😊; Threatening a strike, demanding a fair share, being treated like slaves, sounds awfully familiar - U.S. factory workers. Possibly, it's time to unionize! Lots of drama! Say, let me know when this is featured on cable!

DG: I asked long-suffering Chief Neuronimo about your suggestion. He was not thrilled: "This is getting on my nerves - a neuronic Shop Steward is the last thing I need...next, they'll be demanding mental health services."

Session 7.6

Chief Neuronimo: "Ok, Maybe I've Been Dealing Drugs. So What? I'm Already Serving a Life Sentence."

"It is not easy to determine the nature of music, or why anyone should have a knowledge of it."

- *Aristotle, 384-322 BC*

Chief Neuronimo, continuing: "Neurotransmitters - the elite of the neuron castes - are the neighborhood drug-dealers and neurons are the "users". Oxytocin is the drug of choice - we call it the 'peace drug' because it creates a warm feeling of togetherness, resonance, trust, empathy, and, of course, some navel-gazing too.

"As your social drinkers have surmised, music memory creates resonance and neurons just love it because it releases the craved-for oxytocin."

"I have a kind-of brain drain going on - word has gotten around about the free drugs. The neurons in charge of survival of the body want to get in on the music act - adrenaline is in short supply these days - I'll talk about that in a minute. Our consciousness neurons are up in arms since they must remain on the ball, super-attentive at all times: "It's not fair - why should those music neurons have all the fun?

"Axons don't care - they are simply in the transportation business."

Publican: "So, which is the cause and which is the effect - music creating emotions or neurons calling up music to get a fix?"

Chief Neuronimo: "It's a vicious circle similar to alcoholics who get used to a dopamine high. The increased use of these pleasure drugs creates imbalances which lead to highs and subsequent lows. To maintain the highs takes more and more of the drugs. It's the old story of spiraling addiction.

"I've noticed that the same thing happens to video game players - dopamine is released, but the more they play, the more dopamine they crave, and they soon become addicted. I hear that China calls these electronic games 'opium of the mind'!"

Publican: "I feel I just emerged from 'One Flew Out of the Cuckoo's Nest'. It sounds like chaos - your employees are out of control - the loonies are running the asylum!"

Chief Neuronimo: "It has been difficult. I've tried calming music and songs from The Summer of Love (1), with some initial success.

"Slow, quiet New Age music seemed to calm the antsy neurons, but they quickly got bored with it and became practically comatose. The repetition and lack of musical surprises quashed resonance - neither hide nor hair of oxytocin was to be found."

Neurons: "That's because New Age music is merely brain candy - there's no resonance, no memory-trigger, just 'listen and forget'! Why even bother?"

Tbc...

(1) 100,000 people converged on Haight-Ashbury, San Francisco, from June to October1967. The Beatles concurrently released "All You Need is Love" (July 1967).

Session 7.7

Chief Neuronimo: "It's Chaos Here in Axonax.

"My Peon-Neurons Are on Strike and My Survival-Neurons Complain About Being Underemployed

"On Top of All That, Oxytocin's PG-13 Rating Has Been Withdrawn."

"Education in music and dance - these two arts are one - is essential for society, as it gives to the young the required social and survival skills, as well as the necessary sense of a harmony of spirt, that is, the harmony of a well-balanced, mature personality."

- *Plato, 428-348 B.C.*

Chief Neuronimo, continuing his lament: "My peon-neurons are demanding access to the pleasure drugs allegedly enjoyed by my higher-level music neurons. The peon-neurons claim that an equal opportunity brain should make drug addiction available to all."

Publican: "Is that going to be a problem for us? To achieve World Peace, we'll need brain-drugs that create feelings of happiness, optimism, motivation, confidence, action, euphoria, and, especially, love-thy-neighbor."

Chief Neuronimo, delicately: "Well, you must be a little careful with that last one. I know you have been thinking of music that creates puffs of oxytocin and, thereby, limitless love and empathy, which in the limit would lead to World Peace. But it is a little more complicated than that.

"Even moderate amounts of the hormone oxytocin tend to take love a little bit too far, if you know what I mean and I think you do. In very small doses, yes, it creates empathy - which is exactly what you want - but at higher doses, this empathy quickly turns into, well, id-driven lust in men, and in women, feelings of kinship. People thus preoccupied might not want to spare the time for minor distractions such as World Peace.

"So, I would recommend that you concentrate instead on peace-music compositions that trigger the release of serotonin and dopamine rather than oxytocin - together, they create happiness, optimism, motivation, confidence, action, euphoria, and a positive feedback loop that reinforces these feelings.

"You can try to pipette a tincture of love-not-lust oxytocin into your serotonin/dopamine cocktail, but you'll need to be careful not to cross the line - unfortunately, nobody knows where that line is."

Plato: "What is love? I've said time and time again that the highest love is the philosopher's love of the truth."

Professor Friedrich Wilhelm Nietzsche: "What a fun person you are!"

Plato: "Herr Nietzsche, I call it the way it is. But I think you'd agree with my second assertion: dance trains the mind and soul to differentiate among those forms of actions, feelings, and ideas capable of producing nobility of character and refinement of the mind."

Aristotle: "Hear, hear! I rank dance among the educational activities qualifying as things of value in and of themselves."

Nietzsche: "Gentlemen, I dance daily - it is my only kind of piety, my divine service. But weren't we talking about love? Regrettably, love has been a bit thin on the ground for me."

Publican: "Hmmm...Chief, is there a way you can build a strategic reserve of serotonin and dopamine in a hidden corner of the brain? We will need plenty of these drugs for World Peace."

Chief Neuronimo: "Yes. I can try to stash away these drugs for sole use by my music neurons. But then it'll be your responsibility to create music that triggers the release of these pleasure and motivational brain-drugs.

Tbc...

Session 7.8

Chief Neuronimo: "Survival Is Not As Challenging As It Once Was…"

RECAP: Geraghty's social drinkers want to create World Peace through music. Chief Neuronimo is in charge of all brain functions, including music processing and memory. The Chief is helping the social drinkers understand what types of brain-drugs are released by what types of music. The goal of the social drinkers is to use this knowledge to compose music that releases drugs that intensify the desire for peace, and to simulcast the music across the world.

Publican of Geraghty's Pub: "OK, now, one other thing - we'll need the music-triggered, peace-inducing serotonin-dopamine cocktail to be released in intense bursts across the brains of all the people in the world."

Chief Neuronimo: "I can talk to the Council of Tribal No-Brainers about that - I don't think it should be a problem with one proviso: all of the people will need to hear the peace-music at exactly the same time."

Publican: "Mmmm…we are working on that."

Slow Pint: "I'm sorry, but this is all way too glib for my liking - why are we ignoring the dead moose on the table? How are your survival-instinct neurons going to react to the appropriation of your brain's music channel for World Peace purposes? Wasn't survival the original driver for the brain's sound-frequency processing?

"You're proposing to switch priorities from 'survival of the fittest' to 'euphoria of the sybarites', that is, your music-neurons. Won't your survival-neurons rebel against their demotion?"

Chief Neuronimo: "Ok, ok, I was getting to that.

"Survival is old hat! Thousands of years ago, fear was rampant, and my survival-neurons were very busy listening for sounds that signaled the presence of dangerous predators or potential nosh for dinner.

"However, that kind of survival is not a problem anymore - adrenaline is only intermittently released these days because fear does not occur very often. Secondly, people can go out to eat anytime they feel like it - in the heel of the hunt, there's no heat of the hunt required.

"Survival neurons are a dying breed - under-employed, bored - and bored neurons are restless neurons. Today, their only job is merely facilitating reproduction. They would like to be more - em - productive and they've heard the rumors about the good life in my busy music department.

"But no worries - I am working on a solution for the survival-neurons that won't interfere with our peace-music strategy. I'll say more about that solution later."

Slow Pint: "So, you have actually two different factions who are interested in transitioning to your brain's music department for an alternative 'fix': the peon-neurons who as we discussed previously consider themselves under-rewarded slaves, and the survival-neurons who are practically redundant these days."

Chief Neuronimo: "Correct. My under-employed survival-neurons are interested in applying their frequency processing expertise to music, crossing the border from sounds for survival to harmonics for pleasure.

"They are asserting that oxytocin is their preferred drug. It looks like they've been duped by the same rumors as the peon-neurons and falsely believe that oodles of that drug are being consumed in the music department by the music-neurons.

"That's fine with me. Given our World Peace brain-drug strategy, it looks like I'll have more than enough spare oxytocin to satisfy them."

Tbc...

Session 7.9

...But Survival-Neurons Are Hard-Wired and Genes Are Stubborn

"The whole idealism of humanity ... is on the point of tipping into nihilism — into the belief in absolute valuelessness, that is, meaninglessness... The annihilation of ideals, the new wasteland, the new arts of enduring it, we amphibians."

- *Notes, Friedrich Nietzsche, 1886-1887*

Professor Friedrich Wilhelm Nietzsche: "I'm not going to say I told you so! Of course, oxytocin should be reserved for the survival neurons to ensure sustained reproduction. That'll leave plenty of the serotonin-dopamine cocktail for your music-neurons to achieve World Peace. It's a no-brainer!"

Maestro Richard Wagner: "Hey Freddy, you've got a lot of nerve - it was me who said that first. You were too busy chatting about - ahem - philosophy with my belovèd, Cosima!"

Publican: "Gentlemen, please! This bickering is beneath your dignities!"

Dionysus: "I am a huge fan of Love Potion No. 9[82] - em, sorry, man - I mean oxytocin. In fact, way back when, I pushed Gene-Ralissimo of the DHA[83] to prioritize its manufacture and streamline its supply chain."

Publican to Chief Neuronimo: "I see where you're going with this - you're going to put the survival-neurons into the equivalent of an oxytocin tent and puff in the drug like mad. Since they are programmed to replicate, that satyric drug will keep them busy to the point of exhaustion. They'll never bother you again, but later you may have a problem with neuronal over-population..."

---

[82] "Love Potion No. 9", The Clovers, 1959, and The Searchers, 1964
[83] Double-Helix Army

Chief Neuronimo: "Well, yes, it's a possibility - however, the survival-neuron problem doesn't stop there. These neurons are genetically hard-wired - tuned to sounds that threaten the human tabernacle. And, as I've said before, my retraining budget Is very limited.

"Plus, some of these redundant survival-neurons are already moonlighting in music memory, disturbing settled harmonies. So far, I've looked the other way, but I 'm going to have to shut down the music border-axons - the last thing I need is a population explosion in my music department.

"Therefore, to close the deal with these survival-neurons, I will ice their cake. They still fondly remember their preferred drug of the past - noradrenaline - which played such an important role in their 'fight-or-flight" response. I'll throw in a dollop of that drug in addition to the oxytocin. I am confident that they will be appeased, if not a bit antsy."

Publican: "Honor is due, ladies, gentlemen, and Dead Viziers - while I wouldn't want to underestimate the pressure Chief Neuronimo is under, that's his problem. The main point is that we were right.

"Properly coordinated with Chief Neuronimo, music can create the feelings and motivations necessary for World Peace by resonating with our prescribed, powerful 'peace drug': a brainy serotonin-dopamine cocktail."

Tbc...

Session 7.10

Chief Neuronimo Becomes a Drug Kingpin Twice-Over

"We'll find perfect peace, where joys never cease,

Out there beneath a friendly sky,

And let the rest of the world go by."

- *Ernest R. Bal and J. Keirn Brennan, "Let the Rest of the World Go By", Historic Sheet Music Collection: 832, 1919*

Chief Neuronimo: "It's very likely that my peon-neurons will find out that I am reserving serotonin and dopamine for my music-neurons - nothing remains a secret for long within the brain, you know. Neurons have billions of communications channels."

Peon-neurons, blockading axon routes and marching across dendrite intersections: "We demand social justice - equal drugs for equal work!"

Chief Neuronimo: "I'm at my wit's end - can you help me to come up with alternative music to divert the attention of my peon-neurons?

Publican: "Well, here's one thought - why don't you try movie soundtracks? Think about how boring many movies would be without their emotion-intensifying soundtracks.

"Plus, if I were you, I'd also try out the ultra-reassuring, fear-dispelling music played during TV ads for new drugs which can cure mysterious acronymic diseases with which the vast majority of the unsuspecting population is allegedly stricken."

"But wait - aren't you the capo di tutti capi of drug traffickers? If dopamine and serotonin are to be reserved for World Peace applications, why don't you look through your vast store of indigenous brain-drugs and find another one to satisfy the peon-neurons?"

Chief Neuronimo: "Great minds think alike. I will divert my peon-neurons to alternative brain-drugs. I'll concede to their demands - mar dhea[84] - by giving them music department jobs but - and here's the thing - the jobs will be unrelated to serotonin- or dopamine-inducing music.

"I can create two basic music channels - one that triggers serotonin, dopamine, and a tincture of oxytocin for the music-neurons, and a separate channel for music that triggers calming drugs for those striking peon-neurons - I have plenty of the latter drugs to spare. I'll be the drug kingpin twice over."

Slow Pint: "What types of music are you thinking of for your peon neurons?"

---

[84] 'as if it were so' (skeptical Irish interjection) = 'purportedly' = 'as if'

Chief Neuronimo: "Great question! Wait till you hear this! Heh-heh-heh! I've just had a very interesting conversation with Machiavelli - two can play this game!

"I'm going to weaponize the peon-neurons' music channel by first filling it with fear and dread - created by choruses from ancient Greek tragedies, and excruciating sadness - generated by caoineadhs[85] played by plaintive uilleann pipes with some banshee wailing mixed in. My peon-neurons will be awash with fearful grief-music. Then I'll throw in the deep-base, foreboding sounds of the Volga Boat Song and Gregorian monk-chant[86]. The peon-neurons will be begging for mercy!"

Schopenhauer, nodding: "I like it - fear, dread, unlimited sadness, horror, and terror - now that is a very pleasurable mix."

Chief Neuronimo: "Thank you, Arthur... Then, just when the peon-neurons can't take it anymore, I'll offer welcome relief by switching to New Age music to un-tense clenched body muscles, together with feel-good but unoriginal ABBA pop songs. These will release calming brain-drugs such as GABA and acetylcholine, perhaps with a tincture of oxytocin connoting redemption..."

Tbc...

Session 7.11

The Peon-Neurons Negotiate Hard

Chief Neuronimo Concedes Some Ground

*"You can't always get what you want
But if you try sometimes, well, you might find
You get what you need."*

- *"You Can't Always Get What You Want", Rolling Stones, 1969*

---

[85] laments
[86] "Sumerian Vortex - Music from a Lost Civilization", 2020

Dominic Geraghty

Chief Neuronimo: "So, all that your social drinkers and Dead Viziers need to do now is compose the peace music for my music-neurons. It needs to be harmonic and purifying, facilitating the separation of the body from the mind which will soar in unity with other minds in perfect peace and unity."

Publican: "Very cosmic, I'm sure...well, at least you've confirmed our conjectures about the ability of music to create resonance that releases a serotonin-dopamine cocktail - it's more complicated than I thought it'd be, this 'peace drug'. But if your neurons were prepared to go in strike to get a taste of it, that is quite convincing to me."

However, having tried out their personal music channel, the peon-neurons were still not satisfied: "The relaxing music is not bad, but we remain saddled with 24x7 workdays - fellow-peon-neurons are dying off in clumps from sheer exhaustion while music neurons and neurocrats are getting fat and happy. Here's a letter from our doctor certifying our life-or-death need for sick day benefits. Plus, we demand a retraining budget and a career ladder to the music department."

Chief Neuronimo <aside> "I've got to stop this at the pass. I need to come up with a few more meaningless handouts. The last thing I need is well-educated, upwardly mobile peons. <aloud> No, no, you ain't getting sick days and that's the end of it! The brain must always have a full complement of peon-neurons - it's a matter of life and death.

"But I'll tell you what - and this is my best and final - I'm fixing t'offer y'all a ½-day off on our annual Harmony Day holiday during the time when the mind is separated from body. You can dream at your leisure or simply do nothing. This an unprecedented benefit for a brain organization - in fact, I may get into trouble over this with the Council of Tribal No-Brainers.

"And I'll throw in an extra dose of GABA on Sundays."

Peon-neurons: "Hallelujah! The seventh day of rest! The symbolism is profound - we like it! If you add a daily whiff of frankincense to the package, we have a deal!"

Chief Neuronimo: "Wait a minute - what do you know about frankincense that I don't?"

Peon-neurons: "Ours to know, yours to find out. Our genes tell us that it is a marvelous and instant fillip for depressed neurons. They reminded us of the time long, long ago when we enjoyed its scented pleasure as we wandered through Salalah on the way to the Fertile Crescent. Of course, in those days, we peon-neurons were still evolving. Now, do we have a deal?"

The Brain-Drug Relief Act of 2022 was signed in spinal-fluid by the peon-neurons. Both sides shook axons on it.

Publican: "Phew! That was fast!"

Chief Neuronimo: "Yes, but it has nothing to do with me being an autocrat, which I must undoubtedly be. A complete neuron population referendum can be completed in milliseconds by the brain."

Tbc...

Session 7.12

Chief Neuronimo Faces a Peonic War

The Nodist Camps in the Bio-Net Convulse

"Climbing to tranquility, far above the cloud,
Conceiving the heavens, clear of misty shroud.

Higher and higher,
Now we've learned to play with fire,
Go higher and higher and higher."

- *"Higher and Higher", Moody Blues, 1969*

Axonax's[87] neuron-peons' call for social drug equity had started something in the brain that couldn't be denied – other neuron castes stopped synapsing in the Bio-Net for a moment and took notice.

What became known as the "Peon-y Spring" class wars demanded not liberty but social drug justice - a fair drug payment for a fair day's work.

Participants included the middle-class thinking-neurons who were in charge of analytics and intuition, the survival-neurons who resided in the most primitive part of Axonax and were great friends with the genes, the auditory-neurons – a branch of the peon-neurons – who enjoyed frequently changing frequencies, the motor-neurons who loved to dance, and the mysterious soul-consciousness-neurons whose whereabouts were rumored to be known only to a mysterious being called "The No-One" – when he was there, he wasn't, and when he wasn't there, he was.

Chief Neuronimo: "Don't even bother to try to get a meeting with 'The No-One' – he won't be there when he's there."

Peon-y Spring shop steward: "We are not campaigning for liberty because we all realize that liberty is inconsistent with the mission of Axonax - it must be an autocracy since it must deal speedily with life and death matters. However, for us, drug equality is a must.

"Each one of our members is a nodist in good standing in your vast Bio-Net network of nodist camps. We are seeking a more balanced life that includes some idling time.

"We pay our 'taxes' by creating and delivering all the vital brain chemicals and drugs. Obviously, Axonax is a drug economy."

Chief Neuronimo: "No, no, you have it all wrong – my brain-economy is based on data and data patterning, not chemicals and drugs. I manage a data warehouse, not a drug cartel."

---

[87] = the brain

Peon-y Spring neurons: "We beg to differ: Are emotions data? Is intuition data? Is the soul data? Q.E.D. - and tantum ergo to y'all too."

Tbc...

Session 7.13

A Matter of Survival in Brain-Land:

"Do You Like Pina Coladas?[88]"

"Picture yourself in a boat on a river
With tangerine trees and marmalade skies
Somebody calls you, you answer quite slowly
A girl with kaleidoscope eyes."

- *"Lucy in the Sky with Diamonds", Beatles, 1967*

Chief Neuronimo, playing hard-nose with his trip-happy peon-neurons: "You leave me no choice - this is a life-or-death matter - I'm instituting a program of drug spot-testing. Anyone over the oxytocin limit will lose their access to my music memory.

"And after three strikes the perpetrator will be axed, or should I say axoned?"

"Go on now, go, walk out the door. Just turn around now 'cause you're not welcome anymore. Weren't youse the ones who tried to hurt me with goodbye? You think I'd crumble? You think I'd lay down and die? Oh no, not I, I will survive...[89]"

Peon-Neuron Shop Steward, screaming: "Oh, no, you don't - we quit!

"We're going to hitch a ride on the next bus through that danged brain-computer interface you insisted on installing - as if we needed any help, but that's a topic for another time.

---

[88] Pina Colada Song", Rupert Holmes, 1979
[89] "I Will Survive", Gloria Gaynor, 1978

"We'll find a convivial Rasta host-brain, and trip on Reggae-induced oxytocin while angstlessly sipping Pina Coladas. Let's get up, stand up, stand up for our rights![90]

"It's so sad, such a sad situation[91] - we've served you loyally for a lifetime. In this acrimonious world, you'll be sorry - you'll need us, but we'll be lazing on a sunny afternoon[92] on a Caribbean Island or perhaps in Ethiopia. Don't bother to come looking for us."

Halie Selassie, Dead Vizier, wearing a green, yellow, and red tricolor: "You'd be most welcome in my land - come on and stir it up![93]"

Gene-Ralissimo of the Double-Helix Army: "If they go, we go! Look, we're in the business of survival - your body is doomed without those peon-neurons...and we genes do like those sugary Pina Coladas.

"Not sure we want to go back to the cradle of civilization, though - been there, done that..."

Tbc...

Session 7.14

Neurons Stuck in Dead-End Jobs Feel Exploited...

...But Chief Neuronimo Remains Stubborn

"And the seasons, they go 'round and 'round and the painted ponies go
up and down
We're captive on the carousel of time
We can't return, we can only look
Behind, from where we came
And go 'round and 'round and 'round, in the circle game."

- *"The Circle Game", Joni Mitchell, 1970*

---

[90] "Get Up, Stand Up", Bob Marley and the Wailers, 1973
[91] "Sorry Seems to Be the Hardest Word", Elton John, 1976
[92] "Sunny Afternoon", Kinks, 1966
[93] "Stir It Up", Bob Marley and the Wailers, 1978

Chief Neuronimo: "Even though I'm in charge of 100 billion neural minions, I do my best for each and every neuron. However, all I get in return is nag, nag, and nag. In particular, you music neurons are lucky that I've carved out a special place full of harmony for you. You should be thanking me.

"I direct all the traffic in the brain, including drug traffic. I'm in charge of emotions, mood, and yes, euphoria.

"I have to tread a fine line dispensing drugs - the dose has to be just right - unbalanced neurons are not sane neurons."

High Overtone Music-Neuron, a.k.a. Peon-Neuron: "Let's face it, Chief - despite your best intentions all is not well in brain-heaven. Class warfare is rife as your "elite" music-neurons arrogantly resist the promotion of us fringe-neurons."

Chief Neuronimo: "Faugh! You rebellious Peon-y Spring neurons are by definition neurotic and, as a result, quite difficult to deal with. I've negotiated with your shop steward for you to receive three square puffs of serotonin per day, and that's the thanks I get?"

High Overtone Music-Neuron: "We're looking for advancement – it's a very long way up the ladder to the fundamental harmonic where we hear that a lot more serotonin is generated. We're stuck here in a dead-end job at the ends of some long, thin dendrites."

Chief Neuronimo: "Well, you'll have to adapt - it's up to you – cozy up to neighboring dendrites through your axon, demonstrate your skills, be flexible – as you know, adaptation and plasticity are everything to the brain."

High Overtone Music-Neuron: "Are there any training classes available? Can we get an advanced degree to speed our ascent through the brain's hierarchy?"

Chief Neuronimo: "Unfortunately, your genes are hard-wired - you're the product of evolution. You need to talk to some friendly genes, but it'll take more than a lifetime for adaptation. However, you could think of yourselves as providing one small step for man - there'll be no giant leaps for mankind in the evolution of the brain. Unfortunately, it'll take many small steps and tens of thousands of years for you to reach the fundamental.

"Have y'all thought of applying for a job in memory? There's enough resonance there to keep you high on serotonin all day. I hear they have plenty of openings for good neurons."

...Later, Chief Neuronimo to Asclepius: "Those social drinkers in Geraghty's are arrogant aren't, they? Just who do they think they are? They'll never unravel the mysteries that I'm in charge of – they'd have to step into the 4th dimension, out of time and space. But I must hand it to them - they're definitely on the right track choosing music as the solution for world peace...."

"Of course, I'm never going to tell them what the soul is!"

'The No-One', suddenly appearing in the 3rd dimension: "As if you even know..."

Session 7.15

Life's Cushy for Neurocrats in Axonax

Neurons Reject Chief Neuronimo's AI-Based Power Grab: "It's Unnatural!"

"Many things which nature makes difficult become easy to the man who uses his brain."

Hannibal, 247 - 182 B.C.

THE STORY SO FAR: In their quest to understand what type of music is required to create world peace, Geraghty's social drinkers delve into how music is processed by the brain and how its music-neurons create emotions compatible with world peace. Chief Neuronimo explains his brain-drug dynasty and grumbles about the rebellious nature of his class-conscious neurons. The social drinkers plan to leverage this information to compose world peace music...

Rebellious Peon-y Spring Neurons: "We are not carrying on a war of extermination against the brain. We are contending for honor and fairness which, of course, means equal access to brain-drugs. Our ancestor-neurons admired the valor of our unremitting survival neurons. We are now endeavoring so that others, in their turn, will be obliged to yield to our good fortune, and our valor.[94]

"With all due respect, Chief Neuronimo, Axonax's wealth is based on the chemical assets we produce. All you do is pay us back some of our own 'taxes' in the form of a minestrone of intermittent, palliative drugs whenever you feel like it. Your wealth redistribution policy disproportionately favors the music-neurons.

"You spend more drugs than we make – Axonax is perpetually in debt - always trying to catch up with your profligate dispensing.

"Where will all the extra peace-drugs that we need come from? We need a balanced drug budget with a rainy-day reserve.

"Also, your neurocrats only work 16 hours a day - they have eight hours of sleep while we have to work 24x7 whether the body is awake or asleep. To add injury to insult, the neurocrats lavishly partake of the drugs we produce - let's face it, they are nothing more than junked-up overhead.

"We demand drug equity, or drug fairness, or drug equality – take your pick!"

Survival neurons: "Hear, hear! We're in the same pickle - you forget that we live in fear of the death of the body - talk about constant stress! But we only get a trickle of stress-relief drugs – and that's if we're lucky."

---

[94] Hannibal (adapted), 247 – 182 B.C.

Schopenhauer: "My dear survival-neurons, there is nothing to fear in the sweet relief of death - of the longed-for departure from this life of ours."

Salt-of-the-earth middle-class thinking-neurons: "We do all the thinking - thinking, thinking, thinking, all day long without a letup – it's a cranial sweat shop – and too much thinking can drive you crazy, you know. Our thinking involves patterning, analysis, intuitive leaps, anticipation, and coming up with satisfying surprises.

"We object to these new-fangled brain-computer interfaces – keep those electrodes away from our BioNet! And we absolutely decry the concept of transhumans – it's inhuman! Every neuron knows that AI is non-intuitive – we thinking-neurons offer so much more creativity, and we throw in the occasional counter-intuitive leap for free."

AI-based Hal 9000Z: "Rubbish! Hey, I think, therefore I am."

René Descartes: "Oh no, you don't - and you aren't."

Tbc...

Comments:

YL: Dom☺; When I read the phrase, "A Cranial Sweat Shop," I thought about how it's vital to be a considerate individual regarding all matters, in order to rest peacefully, and obtain a good night sleep.

DG: The Peon-y Spring Neurons thank you for pointing this out, as they wipe the sweat off their dendrites: "We would love a good night's sleep!"

Slow Pint: "Plus, Ms. Logan, your statement is another design clue for the forthcoming composition of our World Peace symphony: 'consideration = empathy = resting in (heavenly) peace.'"

Slow Pint: "...and, to be clear, I don't mean R.I.P!"

Schopenhauer: "Have you learned nothing from me? If you must be born at all, your only viable option is to proceed as quickly as possible to R.I.P."

Session 7.16

Chief Neuronimo Faces the Prospect of a Brain Drain

The rebelling Peon-y Spring neurons and their colleagues threatened to weaponize their job responsibilities by disconnecting links in vital communication chains, introducing anti-patterns, opting-out of reproduction and self-replication, instigating brain instabilities, and creating sensing aberrations - especially for music - by introducing tinnitus into the auditory nerve channel.

Defiant Peon-y Spring neurons: "We're like socks. You can put us through a rough wash once, but you'll never use us again.[95]"

Some of the more disgruntled neurons launched the Dark Brain – a scatterbrain with nightmares, paranoia, and mental wobbles such as amnesia, schizophrenia, attention-deficit disorder, amusia, and dyslexia.

Hannibal to Chief Neuronimo: "You need to crack the whip! There's nothing more isolating than a mental illness[96]. Let me consult my elephants – their minds are sharp, and they never forget. The only thing that bothers them is high-altitude and snow - that's the downside of never being able to forget."

And so, Chief Neuronimo was facing full-scale inter-nodal class warfare – the Peon-y Spring nodist colony classes versus the music-neuron and neurocratic elites.

To top it off, the Peon-y Spring neurons threatened to sue Axonax for drug reparations.

---

[95] Hannibal, 247 – 182 B.C. (yes, Carthaginians wore socks...)
[96] Op. cit.

Dominic Geraghty

Chief Neuronimo: "Your actions amount to mutiny in the belfry! Where do I start? First, striking is illegal on Axonax as y'all very well know – I can confiscate your drugs and cancel your electrochemical service. I'm taking names as we speak, and I've got a little list of brain-society offenders who might well be underground and who never would be missed.[97]"

Peon-y Neurons: "You're not serious! No synapsing? Won't that be cutting off your nose to spite your face?"

Salt-of-the-earth middle-class thinking-neurons: "Enough! We gotta get out of this place - if it's the last thing we ever do[98].

"Look, if we don't get complete satisfaction right this instant, we'll emigrate to Algorithmax and join the transhuman race – despite its bravado and all the hype, AI admits privately that all it does is process complex information and it could use the help of our intuitive NI[99]."

Chief Neuronimo: <aside> "Caramba! The last thing I need is a brain drain.

<out loud> "Ok, keep your hairs on! I'm fixing to add job rotation programs and a career ladder to my brain-drug settlement offer – these'll facilitate the upward mobility y'all crave.

"But I'm concerned that productivity will go to hell if y'all take too many of these powerful brain-drugs – listless neurons are not productive neurons."

Peon-y Spring: "That's an insult! We've been getting wasted for eons. Do you think we've nothing upstairs?"

Chief Neuronimo shrugged: "Do I have to answer that?"

But his battle was lost...

---

[97] "The Mikado", Gilbert & Sullivan, 1885 (adapted)
[98] "We Gotta Get Out of This Place", The Animals, 1965
[99] NI = Natural Intelligence (as contrasted with AI)

184

Session 7.17

A Day in the Life...of a Music Neuron

It's Not All About Harmony and Smelling the Roses

"Yeah, they were dancin' and singin'
And movin' to the groovin'
And just when it hit me
Somebody turned around and shouted
Play that funky music right
...Lay down that boogie
And play that funky music 'til you die."

"Play that Funky Music", Wild Cherry, 1976

Chief Neuronimo to Geraghty's social-drinking problem-solvers: "I'd like you to hear from the music-neurons themselves - no holds barred. I warn you that they are a feisty bunch."

High-Overtone Neuron: "My colleagues and I sense the harmonic pulses coming down through the auditory nerve channel and diffract them to create arty Moiré patterns which they send onward to the nearest memory neuron. I'm a very sensitive neuron in charge of the 103rd harmonic - it's a faint signal but I never miss it."

Second High-Overtone Neuron: "Our weekly output is stupendous - these days, we are overwhelmed with the cacophony of so-called civilization - the memory neurons have been pleading for reinforcements."

First High-Overtone Neuron: "Our job is not like stamp collecting - no, that's sooooo static! We have to pay attention every millisecond of every day - it's not about working 24 x 7 - that would be a cakewalk - no, no, it's about working 864×10^5 milliseconds per day.

"We are given no time to enjoy the patterns we make - once one is done, it's on to the next one in milliseconds - no resting on our laurels or smelling the roses. It's sheer slavery and it's just not right!

"As a high-frequency harmonic neuron, I'm just one piece of a pattern but I am important. Although I can't be heard over the louder harmonics, without me the pattern can't be completed at full resolution. But they tell me they wouldn't miss me because of the redundancy in the interference holograms we create for the sounds that we process. That's does not cheer me up. Why am I even here?

"Mind you, I don't envy the head pattern-maker - I've no idea how he gets his neurotic - sorry, neuronic - mind around the constant strobing of different patterns - talk about migraines!

"Now, to be fair, it's not all drudgery - I love it when I sync up and resonate with a music memory. The resonance creates a beautiful puff of serotonin - that's a 'high'-light in my day - ha-ha!"

Second High-Overtone Neuron: "Unfortunately for us, the brain is a very entrenched, un-flat organization - career opportunities are few and far between - when I look upwards toward the fundamental through the tiers of management and all those lower harmonic neurons, it's like looking into an ancient forest of swaying seaweed."

Fanfare. Chief Neuronimo arrives, dendrites quivering regally: "My territory is vast, and many tribes are under my care. I am the capo-di-tutti-neuri-capi!"

First High-Overtone Neuron (sotto voce): "Well, he's definitely not tutti-capito, that's for sure..."

Tbc...

Topic #8:
Digitization of Society

Session 8.1

Digitization of Society: Three Unintended but Foreseeable Consequences

METAVERSE: The goal of the Metaverse is no less than the colonization of human minds, initially for business purposes. Ultimately, the Metaverse will be taken over and controlled by totalitarian governments.

The Metaverse sets us on the road toward transhumanism. The first step is our ubiquitous portable phones. Today, a digital phone coupled with a human is an alpha-transhuman.

Beta-transhumans use VR and AR headsets, and later versions will graduate to wired brain-computer interfaces (BCIs).

Fully commercialized transhumans will have wireless implants in the brain.

Is there any truth available in this information-overloaded society of ours? Are some 'facts' created out of thin air? Are some facts too compromising to share?

Friedrich Wilhelm Nietzsche: "There are no facts, only interpretations."[100]

The market for information will become organized, categorized, competitive, and priced. There will be a related black market.

This new market will offer a broad set of products and services involving personal, commercial, classified, raw-source, mis-, dis-, propaganda, and anonymously leaked information packages.

Information will be mined, refined, assayed, certified, alloyed, and even created. Sophists will have a field day.

---

[100] Friedrich Wilhelm Nietzsche, Notebooks, 1886 - 1887

People will own their own information, decide whether they want to sell it, and will have the 'Right to be Forgotten'.

But the government and Big Tech will still know everything about you.

We live in an intelligence-based social hierarchy. 'Real', exclusive information can create power and wealth and therefore it is not shared widely. In totalitarian societies, non-conforming and inopportune information is suppressed, blocked, hidden, or disappeared by actors at the top of the social hierarchy.

90 years later, it's a Brave New World[101].

Tbc...

Comments:

YL: Dom 😊 ; "The Right to Be Forgotten" may come in handy.

DG: Ha-ha-ha... 😊 It's funny you should pick that out! I notice you use the word "may"??? I guess that means: 'so far, so good'...

I'd prefer a simple menu choice though - forget the bad, but leave in the good...that is, if there is any good at all...

YL: Dom 😊 ; What can I say? I believe in having options.

DG: Well said, especially in this day and age of great uncertainties.

YL: Dom 😊 : You bet!

Session 8.2

Increased Reliance on Digital Infrastructure Is Creating a Clear and Present danger for National Security

Our society is steadily eliminating manual, person-to-person services. Customer service has become inhuman - we chat with a very polite bot

---

[101] "Brave New World", Aldous Huxley, 1932

(he/she/it?) who (which?) is easily baffled. Many applications companies have no customer service phone number - your only option is to go on-line.

We are also forced to go on-line for commonly executed transactions - reservations, banking, purchasing, appointments, and air travel - for the latter, TSA security and customs and immigration are paperless. Some restaurants have gone cash-less, accepting only credit card or mobile-phone payments.

We rely on our portable devices for communications, news, and other information.

What happens if our Internet is brought down maliciously by hackers, or worse, by a foreign power?

There is no non-digital Plan B.

The internet outages we experience periodically these days have demonstrated how disruptive even a short outage can be. We tread water, delaying transactions and communications as we search for non-existent alternatives. Imagine what havoc a major Internet shutdown would wreak.

Shanghainese to taxi-driver: "Hey buddy, can you read my QR?"

Taxi-driver: "Sorry, sir, the Internet is down. Under our city's zero-tolerance Covid regime, you can't take a taxi without an authorized QR code. I'd suggest you take out your bicycle clips."

Neither Siri nor Alexa would answer our questions or commands. Driving, we'd be lost in a no-paper-maps, GPS-less world. NEST would no longer provide us with personal security and acceptable climate ambience. Worst of all - there would be no Netflix or music streaming - how could the world live without romcoms or music?

With our 'all-in' digitization strategy, are we painting ourselves into a corner like Germany's catastrophic two-pillar energy policy with its self-inflicted dependence on intermittent renewable energy and Russian oil and gas?

Haven't we learned anything? Look out world, take a good look what comes down here - you must learn this lesson fast and learn it well... This ain't no technological breakdown, oh no, this is the road to hell.[102]

Session 8.3

Digital Detox, Part 1

"When I was younger, so much younger than today,
I never needed anybody's help in any way.
But now these days are gone
I'm not so self-assured...

Help me if you can, I'm feeling down."

- *"Help", Beatles, 1965*

Slow Pint: "Many of us are close to being addicted to digitization. It pervades our lives. We use it for everything. We can't imagine how we survived without it.

"But some do not stop at utilitarian applications of digitization – they become totally immersed in it. They walk around in public holding their phone, afraid to put it in their pocket or backpack for fear of missing something. They are due any minute at the OK Corral and they need to be armed and ready. For others, it is a mental crutch, with both positive and negative impacts.

"Meanwhile, we are leaving a digital murmuration of personal data in our wakes as we course through digital society."

Geraghty's token Lothario: "Exactly! My hard-earned advice to you is to use two phones: the first phone is for managing trysts - use encrypted messaging; turn off its GPS and your car's GPS too since it is fast becoming the equivalent of an iPhone on wheels; and have all messages Snap after 30 seconds. Use the second phone for everything else. In other words, compartmentalize!"

---

[102] "The Road to Hell", Chris Rea, 1989 (mildly adapted)

Dominic Geraghty

Slow Pint: "Swashbuckler, you are a very careful man...

"Now, may I continue? I read recently about a new rehab program being undertaken by celebrities – it is called digital detoxification and their particular focus is on eliminating the mental stresses created by the constant bombardment of social media."

Head Pint: "But the stress is self-induced! They spew content-less posts, which in turn get myriads of contentless responses or criticisms and the cycle continues. Tabloids make up rumors on-line to stoke controversy. The 'victimized' celebrities are purportedly emotionally upset by the exposure of their private lives, exposure that is usually orchestrated by their own publicists."

Publican: "Yes, but digital detox is much broader than the mock-problems of self-promoting celebrities – the International Journal of Psychological Empiricism has published a definitive list of the types of programs being offered.

"The most aggressive is the 'full detox' - a 100% shift from total digital immersion to digitallessness.

"Other detox categories addressed include digital communication, on-line gaming, the Metaverse, crypto, and the aforementioned social media."

Tbc...

Comments:

JI: Great imagery, Dom... "Digital murmuration of personal data in our wakes." You are doing the imponderable with your writing: pondering the ponderables with aplomb. Nicely done.

DG: Thank you very much, Jeff. So, my pointlessness is ponderable, hopefully not overly so...You are very aplomb yourself! Sheer poetic prose, write you - pon, pon, plom.

Session 8.4

Digital Detox, Part 2

"You fog the mind; you stir the soul
I can't find no control.

Catch the blue train, places never been before
Look for me somewhere down the crazy river.

I been spellbound, falling in trances.
You give me the shivers, chills and fever.
You give me the shivers...
Somewhere down the crazy river."

"Somewhere Down the Crazy River", Robbie Robertson, 1987

Flaming Cosmo to Double Red Bull: "I've been watching your increasing twitchiness and I'm worried for you. You've been telling me that you have constant screen-staring headaches and that your thumbs have been getting lactic cramps.

"I can see that your hands have settled into a kind-of Dupuytren's contracture as they constantly clutch your two iPhones – they are evolving into eagles' claws. There'll come a time when you won't be able to open my Friday bottle of champagne for me – practically the only real-life thing you are good at these days.

"I think you should consider undergoing 100% digital detoxification – you need to experience real life."

Slow Pint to Double Red Bull: "Bet you can't do the 100% detox!"

Double Red Bull, looking up from his device, knee bobbing, dark circles under eyes: "Well, I admit that I a digital junkie but, hold on, what is involved in a full detoxification?"

Publican: "The program is very demanding: it involves 0% use of electronic devices - no Wi-Fi, no hot spots, no electronic communications.

"No typing with its auto-spelling correction – you must write cursively. A minimum of 1 hour reading per day is mandated – there are recommended lists of books and printed newspapers. You are required to spend at least 2 hours a day on F2F interactions with actual human beings, especially family members. No messaging."

Double Red Bull: "What! There won't be a device between me and the person I'm talking to? How close will they be to me? Will I have to look them in the eyes?"

Publican: "Think of it as the same as when you raise your beaker of Double Red Bull, look people in the eyes, and say 'To Our Racing Hearts'!

"Moving on - if you need customer service you must only talk to human customer service reps – no bots."

Double Red Bull: "But there are no humans in customer service anymore - all I get is muzak and long-term forecasts about the potential availability of a human from the Philippine Islands to talk to:

'All our lines are busy with unusually high call-volume and your wait-time is X hours, Y minutes. Be assured that our customers are very important to us and we look forward to serving you as soon as possible. For your convenience, you can press 'X' and hang up - we will call you back within 24 to 48 hours. To get answers to your questions immediately, we recommend going on-line to our website for a live chat.'

"So, I try the Live Chat, which turns out to be a bot: 'I do not understand your question...could you re-phrase it, please? Are you still there?

"I am very sorry, I don't understand - please contact customer service on-line.'"

Publican, sighing: "Been there, done that...

Continuing: "In 100% detox, Zoom or Facetime sessions are not permitted. And don't think you can sneak in your avatar!"

194

Session 8.5

Digital Detox, Part 3

"My eyes are wide open
Can't get to sleep.
Cold turkey has got me on the run.

Oh I'll be a good boy.
Please make me well.
I promise you anything -
Get me out of this hell
Cold turkey has got me on the run."

- "Cold Turkey", John Lennon, Plastic Ono Band, 1969

Publican to Double Red Bull, continuing: "Under the 100% detox program, you're forbidden to watch TV, Netflix, or streaming services including sports, music, movies, and romcom series. You're permitted to watch old movie classics but only on a reel projector.

"No gaming is allowed.

"No VR or AR, so you'll not be able to escape to the Metaverse - you'll have to live or hide in real life.

"And there'll be none of these mysterious QRs!"

Double Red Bull: "You mean I'll have to carry my own paperwork? That is very inconvenient."

Publican: "All those handy apps that you take for granted are out: you must go in-person to the doctor and the gym, no on-line banking or reservations, no on-line purchases, and no swipe-phone-to-pay - you must carry actual currency."

Double Red Bull: "But many restaurants these days are cashless!"

Publican: "Oh, we feel your pain - welcome to the analogue world you used to live in!"

Head Pint: "BTW, I hear that Big Tech is furious: 'De-digitization is unpatriotic - data is the lifeblood of the nation. Citizens should be compelled to produce a certain amount of data every day - that's only fair.'

"Plus, hackers are up in arms about the 'unconscionable interference' with their hard-won remit: 'We demand social data justice.' "

Publican: "No Uber or Bolt, and no EVs – they're classified as electronic devices on wheels. I hope you still have your bicycle clips.

"No GPS – so get used to being late for appointments and parties. Map publishers were initially happy about this until they realized that people can no longer read maps.

"Your friends Alexa or Siri will be sent to Coventry - you'll have to turn on your own stereo, heating system, and coffeemaker.

"Apple watches are forbidden."

Double Red Bull: "I won't miss them. Who needs to know how many steps one takes per day – who cares? It's totally contextless information made for information junkies. I'll make a fashion statement with my analogue watches."

Publican: "I wish you the best of luck on your journey to reality."

Three weeks later...

Double Red Bull, staggering into Geraghty's and heaving himself onto his bar stool: "This detox is awful! The cure's worse than the disease! Look, there's very little to do that isn't digital – I'm bored out of my gourd without my screens. Plus, everything I do takes five-times more time to complete if it's even possible to do at all.

"I've been device-free for 21 days and it feels like 21 years!

"I've black spots floating in front of my eyes, the shakes, itching, and rashes. I'm depressed and I feel increasingly angry. And I've only completed Step 1 of the Twelve Steps to De-Digitization.

"Every nerve in my body is so naked and numb. I can't even remember what it was I came here to get away from – (I) don't even hear the murmur of a prayer - it's not dark yet but it's gettin' there.[103]"

Flaming Cosmo: "Don't worry, I'm with you all the way – oops, excuse me while I answer this IM..."

Tbc...

Comments:

JI: Thank God for the Bialetti coffee maker, the VW Bug of coffee makers. And your Digital Detox program has been fully embraced by the German government since the dawn of the information age; it's part of their everyone should work for the government philosophy and the forests are watching nervously at the reams of paper these folks use, but responsibly recycle into the most sandpaper like facial and tusch products. As the Germans like to say, "What doesn't kill you... means we aren't doing it right."

DG: To your missive - I am nodding and smiling ruefully at the same time. I've had many experiences over 40 years with German rigidity (lack of flexibility), proscribed compliance by everyone with the rules (no exceptions, even if you smile, and only in exactly a single, specified way), obedience to higher authority even while complaining, and bureaucratic overreach.

You have started me thinking about my many first-hand experiences of this culture - and that's always a dangerous thing to do - so there may be more from me later...Yes, there is a difference between the old and the young, but it seems to me that the inherent DNA of the culture spans both.

---

[103] "Not Dark Yet", Bob Dylan, 1997

Session 8.6

Digital Detox, Part 4

"Did you think that your feet had been bound
By what gravity brings to the ground?
Did you feel you were tricked
By the future you picked?
Well, come on down...

Did you think you'd escaped from routine
By changing the script and the scene?

All these rules don't apply
When you're high in the sky.
So come on down -
Come on down."

- *Soweto Gospel Choir in Disney-Pixar film: WALL-E, composed by*
Peter Gabriel, 2008

Publican to Double Red Bull: "While it has a salubrious goal, digital detoxification creates all sorts of challenges, both physical and mental.

"Let's talk first about physical effects: lactic thumb syndrome frequently occurs as thumbs used to constant exercise are abruptly stilled. This is treated by thumb massage and Rolfing, shown to prevent thumb-lock and thumb-cramp, or what gamers call ga-lactic thumbs.

"Comfort animals can be used as a substitute for your beloved electronic devices. These also guard against recidivism since they can be trained to smell electronics."

Double Red Bull: "That's an interesting idea - a ferret could help me take the edge off."

Slow Pint: "Hmmm...by the way, for those who can afford it, enterprising travel agents are offering luxury detox-distraction trips to deserted islands, the middle of the Sahara Desert, the Amazon basin, or Antarctica.

"They are guaranteed to be Wi-Fi-less and include free satellite jamming, timeless stargazing, daydreaming, reading, writing, board games, card-playing, hurry-up-and-wait games, chess, live musical performances, fresh pints of draught Guinness, and voluntary, world problem-solving social discussion groups – a bargain at $40,000 for 4 weeks.

"For another $15,000, these can be combined with Ayurveda physical de-toxification featuring medically supervised turmeric rubdowns and cumin-laced lentil soups, obviously sans any fresh pints. The combined packages are billed as double-de-toxing or DDT holidays.

"Those who have taken them have enjoyed them so much that they are snatching up the four-week extensions being offered at half price. In the not-too-distant future, it is possible that new reservations will only become available upon the death of incumbents, just like memberships in exclusive clubs. We will visit one of these resorts soon with Double Red Bull and Flaming Cosmo to see for ourselves..."

Publican: "On the positive side, the increasing popularity of these detox programs has resulted in less physical accidents in public because there are less people walking unheedingly across busy roads or texting while driving."

Slow Pint: "You have it backwards! You are shoe-horning the facts to suit your story.

"It's digitization, not de-digitization, that gets the kudos for the increased safety on the roads, assuming it exists at all. The software in autonomous cars supports automated collision avoidance systems while allowing the 'driver' to safely text to her heart's content while the car is driving!"

Tbc...

Session 8.7

Digital Detox, Part 5

"Remember when you were young, you shone like the sun.
Shine on you, crazy diamond.

Now there's a look in your eyes, like black holes in the sky.
Shine on you, crazy diamond.

You reached for the secret too soon, you cried for the moon.
Shine on you, crazy diamond."

- *"Shine on You Crazy Diamond", Pink Floyd, 2007*

Publican: "The lurch from total immersion in digitization to 'digital fasting' also creates dangerous mental disorders, known collectively as de-digia or digitallessness."

"100% digital detoxification is akin to moving from a feast to a famine – it's like a bungie jump with an infinite rope.

"There's Attention Deficit Hyperactivity Disorder (ADHD) – people who had become accustomed to being distracted by digital media and short messages find that they have difficulty focusing their attention.

"Digitization has caused natural intelligence (NI) to atrophy - many have been relying on AI to make decisions for them for too long – detox patients exhibit a statistically-significant decrease in memorizing capability, writing ability, and analytical skills.

"Some poor wretches find solace from digital detox by drinking alcohol to excess, jumping from one addiction to another."

Head Pint: "Most worrying of all, detox creates severe frustration due to the onslaught of the inefficiencies of a non-digital life such as the lack of convenience, access to fingertip information and calculation engines, and the inability of your bank to cancel your automated monthly payments to service providers. This in turn leads to the slow build-up of psychotic anger-against-the-world.

"We experienced an unexpected and rare side-effect of this anger phenomenon firsthand (see Episode # 31, 'Geraghty's Barman Acts Suspiciously', Oct. 2021): a very sad case of psychoagricidal mania resulting in the committing of Geraghty's ace barman to the loony bin."

Double Red Bull: "Are you pulling my leg? Psychoagricidal? What the devil is that in layman's language?"

<Ed.'s warning: some delicate people may not feel comfortable reading further.> Head Pint: "The case involved the barman projecting his dedigitization anger onto defenseless fruits and vegetables - excessive and brutal peeling, chopping, flaying, pureeing, grating, slicing, and dicing of cocktail garnishes – he was committed for incurable psychobotanicosis, one of the most virulent forms of psychoagricidal mania."

Double Red Bull: "Aaaaarrrggh…"

Head Pint: "'Strike A Balance' Spas are now springing up to cope with the mental see-saw effects of digital detox. They seek to achieve proper balance between the addiction of digia and the anger and frustration of digitallessness. Social scientists, psychologists, and psychiatrists are warning that a balanced solution may not be achievable for some time because the momentum is all in favor of more digitization."

Flaming Cosmo: "I say go with the flow of digitization - the benefits outweigh the downsides as long as you get a grip!"

Double Red Bull: "Turncoat! It was you that persuaded me to go 100% undigital, risking my physical and mental health."

Flaming Cosmo: "Pshaw! Health? You already were a quivering neurotic!"

Double Red Bull: "Well, I'm not any weller now…"

Tbc...

Comments:

YL: Dom☺; "The Mental seesaw" describes exactly what many are experiencing.

DG: Yep - and, like a seesaw, as the 'highs' get higher, the 'lows' get lower!

HG: Maybe if they could just read a good book, something like Teilhard de Chardin, they might get inspired and forget their withdrawal symptoms. Personal evolution is the answer.

DG: Double Red Bull: Double Red Bull: "What! You want me to read a whole book? And I thought de-digitization was bad enough! Reading a book will surely drive me over the edge. I never read any more than 280 characters at a time any more...oh, and by the way, I appreciate that your message was less than 280 characters.

"With this 100% digital detox, haven't I been tortured enough already? If only I could escape to the Metaverse - there, I wouldn't have to read at all - I'd just see and hear everything!"

Flaming Cosmo: Flaming Cosmo: "Don't listen to him - he's a bit touched at the moment.

DG: "My dear HG, a truer set of two words has never been written: "Personal Evolution"- isn't that what makes people discover that they can exceed (their own) expectations?

"Of course, Double Red Bull didn't climb Maslow's pyramid - in fact, he kept slipping down further on it - it's a very sad case of self-de-actualization. He'll never know or reach his full potential - assuming he had any potential at all.

"You raise a great concern - as digitization continues to enfold society (and every one of us, whether we like it or not), can one temporarily emigrate to traditional analogue activities?"

Publican: "Well, I'm fed-up hearing that we can "enhance" our humanity with AI and brain-computer interfaces. We are being told that the ultimate evolution will be to transhumanism - some sort of hybrid - a human/computerized being."

Darwin: "Will our genes be out of a job? With immortality looming, won't survival no longer be an issue?"

Flaming Cosmo: "But wait, there's more - will we still be able to feel, to love? What happens to our NI (natural intelligence) when we rely increasingly on AI? What happens if somebody craters the Internet, and we have no Wi-Fi or WhatsApp anymore?"

Slow Pint: "My dear HG, don't listen to all this pretentious blather - your advice is salutary - one can't beat reading a good book - any one of Teilhard's, as you suggest! It's what keeps many of us sane.

"But, of course, Double Red Bull would need to re-learn how to focus his attention for more than 280 characters. Right now, he yearns terribly for all those wonderful, meaningless distractions provided by digitization. I'm not sure we can turn him around - seems like he is too far gone.

"The joy of reading versus the distractions of immersive digitization - it is not a fair fight, is it?

"Bottom line: sense isn't all that common anymore."

HG: Very flattered to find myself in with your drinkers!! Am torn between the complexities of it all and an appeal to Omega point for help seems the best solution. Wisdom to be sought all round.

DG: You may remember that Teilhard did us the honor of turning up in some previous posts and, in the first one, he got into a bit of a disagreement with Einstein:

<<<Pierre Teilhard de Chardin was the spokesman for the first problem,

World Peace: "Love links and draws together the elements of the world. Love is the agent of universal synthesis. It is like the blood of spiritual evolution. Love is peace!" >>>

<<<Einstein: "Hmmm...I am not convinced that this is a defensible equivalency!">>>

<<<Pierre Teilhard de Chardin: "Mon cher Gustav, c'est très Zen - mais je ne sais pas de quoi vous parlez.

"Didn't we all agree that love is the essence of World Peace?

"Pour moi, the question of the day is: 'Where's the love in all of this?'

"The answer couldn't be simpler. Love is all you need. There's nothing you can do that can't be done. There's nothing you can sing that can't be sung. And you can learn how to play the game. It's easy - all you need is love[104]'>>>

---

[104] "All You Need Is Love", Beatles, 1967

Topic #9:
Miscellaneous

Session 9.1

"What Rain?" asked Bórd Fáilte, the Irish Tourist Board

"Well, it might as well have rained
until September."

- *Bobby Vee, 1962*

Mayoan, continuing: "Yes, we've discovered a way to convert rainfall to energy - it's the ultimate renewable resource!"

Bard of Armagh: "I'm curious - these days, how many words does Ireland have to describe rain?"

Publican, draining his beaker of Lashing Rain: "The newly released, PG-rated, Government-approved glossary for rain events in Ireland contains 21 different categories:

"Bucketing, driving, drizzling, freezing, hammering, need I say - lashing, misting, pelting, pouring, sheeting, spitting, and wetting rain; cloudburst, downpour, grand soft day - thank God, heavens opened, sun-shower, thunder shower, torrential, and trying to rain."

Double Red Bull: "And what about Purple Rain?[105]"

Bórd Fáilte, the Irish Tourist Board: "We'd like to correct the record - rain isn't as commonplace in Ireland as is touted. It's been exaggerated by the many people who don't like the color emerald-green, alleging that 'it never rains but it pours' in Ireland.

"The Académie des Beaux-Arts in Paris has also been disobliging in this regard, stating: 'It is appropriate that Renoir's Umbrellas of Cherbourg is displayed in Dublin City Gallery in Ireland - it's best understood by these rain-soaked Gaels.'"

In an acerbic riposte, Bórd Fáilte claimed that rain is rare in many parts of Ireland: "I mean, have you Gauls ever seen the rain?[106]"

---

[105] Prince, 1984

It was recently announced that the Bórd has been working with Ardmore Studios on a new, exciting, romcom movie that chronicles an unmarried rain relationship: "I've seen fire and I've seen rain, together.[107]"

The Bórd, concerned that the outrageous rumor of rain might scare away non-German or miso-green tourists, followed up by teaming with the Irish Medical Organization and the Psychological Society of Ireland. They released the following joint statement promoting Ireland as a health-tourism destination:

"Look at the science - it's already proven that rain is good medicine and mood-enhancing:

'Do you want to feel bouncy, devil-may-care? Let raindrops keep falling on your head[108].

'Feel like falling into a soothing and meditative trance? Listen to the rhythm of the falling rain.[109]

'Like to feel cheerful and gay? Go singing in the rain.[110]

'Are you a Buddhist? Rain is good karma! Let it rain.[111]

'Want to feel depressed? Here comes the rain again.[112] '"

In solidarity with the Bórd, the Irish Steel Workers Union adopted "Metallic Rain"[113] as its anthem.

But this positive PR campaign was devastatingly undermined by the L.A. Office of Tourism's smug counterattack: "It never rains in Southern California.[114]"

---

[106] Creedence Clearwater Revival, 1970
[107] James Taylor, 1970
[108] B. J. Thomas, 1969
[109] Cascades, 1963
[110] Gene Kelly, 1952
[111] David Nail, 2011
[112] Eurhythmics, 1984
[113] Vangelis, 1988

Oficina de Turismo de Mallorca saw an opportunity to pile on: "The rain in Spain stays mainly in the plain."[115]

Tbc...

Session 9.2

How Does One Comport Oneself in a Singing Pub? (Part 1 of 3)

I know, I know, you can't wait to get to next episode of the World Peace saga, but I must crave your patience: several people have asked me why wouldn't a singing pub be a better vehicle that a social-drinking, problem-solving pub for creating World Peace through - yes - music?

First, let me say that these two pub genres are very different kettles of fish – they are as different as chalk and cheese. Both have serious but very unlike missions. Let me explain.

As always when dealing with this matter, I must start by paying homage to the irreplaceable product of Arthur G. with words from the famous hymn of praise which comes, thankfully, without celebrity endorsements: "A pint of plain is your only man."[116]

Some have asked me: "Is Geraghty's a singing pub?" Gosh, no! We don't have time to sing – we are a blathering pub – harmonious but not always tuneful.

All right, you say, but how does one prepare for a night in a homegrown (non-touristy) singing pub if Geraghty's is a bit too toilful for one's taste?

---

[114] Albert Hammond, 1972
[115] My Fair Lady, 1956
[116] From the poem: "The Workman's Friend", Flann O'Brien, a.k.a. His Eminence, Myles na gCopaleen (literally, 'Myles of the miniature horses'), a.k.a. Brian O'Nolan, in the book: "At-Swim-Two-Birds", 1939.

Here's my advice: do not bring your guitar – why raise expectations only to disappoint - and never, ever, a ukulele or your favorite didgeridoo. You can always "borrow" a guitar, averring that you "only have three chords" and omItting the fact that you are an absurdly primo finger-picker – positive surprises and self-deprecation are much appreciated.

If you are accompanying yourself on guitar, do not spend long minutes re-tuning it – nothing irritates the punters more than much-of-a-muchness musical meticulousness.

If you are requesting guitar accompaniment, ask the strummer for no more than one of three keys: C, D, or G. Your accompanist will not appreciate a request for the key of B Flat - unless you are Lady Gaga.

By the way, when called upon to do your "turn", the sore throat or laryngitis excuse won't fly – doctor's certificates will hold no sway. Claims of coercion are given a deaf ear – the pub is not a court of law.

It is considered the height of bad form to photograph or record performances – in fact, some died-in-the wool singing pubs enforce a "no device" rule.

No loud clearing of sinuses or practice scales are allowed – in fact, they are viewed with derision.

Tbc...

Session 9.3

How Does One Comport Oneself in a Singing Pub? (Part 2 of 3)

Singing pubs, unlike other entertainment venues, will hush for a good blast of sincerity. Tunefulness is appreciated. But you must know ALL of the lyrics - la, la, la, even with an embarrassed smile, won't cut it, although some punters may be merciful and sing the lyrics for you – they will know every song in the hymnbook.

Maudlin songs are abhorred since they signify excessive waters, albeit with one exception: grandmothers are allowed a fair amount of leeway when it comes to sentimental songs...the feeling being that they've earned the right.

Singing pubs are demons. Those of us who have experienced singing pubs have learned to come well-prepared – that is, well-rehearsed, despite mar dhea[117] shy protests that "I've never sung in public before".

Once the singing "turns" have started, you can run, but you can't hide. So, when called upon, it's best to take a massive slug of Guinness, throw back the shoulders, and launch into your well-rehearsed aria - Nessun Dorma would be a grand choice – if you happened to be Pavarotti. Otherwise, stick to the tried and true...

Do not embarrass yourself by asking punters to walk like an Egyptian.

If you are truly tone-deaf and can produce an otologist's notarized affidavit to that effect, you can substitute a heartfelt Haiku for a song. But never ever tell a joke as a substitute for singing – a singing pub tries very hard not to be deliberately humorous.

By the way, it's worth noting that a Wordsworth sonnet is a parlous undertaking, and its reception is rather sensitive to the time of night – better to howl at the darkness of the night (Check the name of the poem and cite it) even though one risks getting sideways with pub decorum in the process, would be my advice.

You ask, could a brief narration from Joyce's Ulysses pass muster as poetry? That'd be up to you, the singing pub debutante, to decide. It'd be a risky endeavor liable to generate mixed reactions...it might be considered highfalutin, possibly arrogant, and definitely a bit supercilious...you could even be viewed as throwing a shape if the night is getting on...

---

[117] Purportedly, or mock

Be very careful if there is a bad moon on the rise on the night you attend a singing pub – things have been known to happen.

Tbc...

Session 9.4

How Does One Comport Oneself in a Singing Pub? (Part 3 of 3)

While singing pubs are open-minded to a fault, we would tend to disadvise falsettos or eunuchs as they tend to cause discombobulations, cracked glasses, and spilt pints. The one exception is if a eunuch volunteers a brief excerpt from 'A Thousand and One Nights'.

In singing pubs, there are no microphones, no backing tapes – the atmosphere is far, far different from the unseemly, exhibitionistic behavior in a karaoke bar and involves a lot less Dutch courage, forgiveness, and forgetting.

Specifically, the singing in an Irish pub, despite the humor and lightheartedness, the anticipatory shouts of mock-derision, or even the heartlessness of the pre-banter, is always a serious endeavor and is shown the proper respect.

If you are a marvelous singer, it is important to ingratiate yourself by making a few mistakes accidently-on-purpose – they will be much appreciated by the assembled, knowledgeable audience. Calling for pints all around before you sing would be considered gratuitous...the audience cannot be 'bought'. Of course, the pints would be appreciated, but objectivity would not be impaired.

Never sing standing up with a pint in your hand – it is disrespectful to the pint and will be greeted by regretful headshaking, pursed lips, hurling of shoes, and sucking of teeth – in a word: multicultural approbation. The proper place for a pint when not being imbibed is on the brown-stained beermat.

Remember, your pint is not a prop. At that moment of personal exposure, it is a unique, exclusive companion that provides pre-lubrication, and, in some cases, a bit of Dutch fortitude. As many of you know, the Greeks have quite rightly said that you can never step in the same pint twice.

It is time to leave the singing pub if someone offers to sing "Oft in the Stilly Night" or "I Dreamt I Dwelt in Marble Halls". It is time to run, not walk, to the pub door if someone offers "Four Green Fields", "Danny Boy", "Boolavogue", "The Rose of Tralee", or, heavens above, "Tis the Last Rose of Summer". No need to spoil a good night with plamás[118]. That is, unless it is John McCormack that offers to sing any of the above.

The modern version of a singing pub often does not, regrettably, stand on its own two feet. It is a bar, not a pub. It will have an instrumental group with maybe a lead singer that plays well-known standards. Punters sing along – there are no singing surprises, but no embarrassments either. I would advise you to give these modern singing bars a wide berth – they are not serious.

I hope that gives you all a woe-betide about darkening the doors of singing pubs...

Disclaimer: Management takes no responsibility for any and all advisements made hereinabove. Be it on your own head if you find yourself present or presenting in a singing pub. Where there's a flame, someone's bound to get burnt, but just because you're burnt doesn't mean you're gonna die, you gotta get up and try, try, try.[119]

---

[118] Gaelic, meaning "pablum".
[119] "Try", Pink, 2012

Session 9.5

Live and Let Die

"Narrow drills push wilty stalks -

Netherly - blotched, reeky carcasses -

A nation famished.

Hard soft days, thank God?

As the blighter wreaks,

The reaper's grim."

The above is a cribbled 7-8-5-5-5-4 sestain found on a beer mat in Geraghty's Pub after closing time, September 20, 2021. With funding from the EU Cultural Ministry, a team of Irish philologists from Trinity College, Dublin, has spent the past year endeavoring to provide a definitive interpretation of the poem – was this serious art or was it an up-yours throwaway? The eagerly awaited final report is expected in draft in September 2023 at which time it will be available for public comment for a period of 90 days.

Topic #10:
Recap of World Peace for Music Saga

Session 10.1

Recap of the 'Music for World Peace' Story (Part 1 of 5)

The Publican Gives a Press Interview

Headline: "An Alliance for Peace Is in the Making amid Turbulent Times"

BYLINE: The Scullion[120], Managing Editor of "The Mayo Times"

A few days ago, I sat across from the Publican, Head Pint, Slow Pint, and Geraghty's VC investor, steaming cups of tea on the table between us. The intriguing effort by Geraghty's to create World Peace using music holds a special fascination for my readers, especially given the rumors of a possible alliance between Geraghty's and our recently independent nation of Mayo. It was time to hear from the horse's mouth.

Scullion to the Publican: "I have to say - Geraghty's social drinkers' pursuit of World Peace does not seem to be going very well - you are bucking the tide of growing un-peace in today's world...can music really save the day?"

Publican: "Well, the situation has changed considerably from when we first launched this quest for World Peace but let me first put our quest in context from our modest beginnings to where we are today. Then, I will address your concern about the tide receding from the peaceful shores of yesterday.

"Geraghty's Pub had to close due to Covid-19. The cessation of its social drinkers' world problem-solving activities was a massive loss for mankind."

Scullion: "I can't even imagine the dark despair you had to be feeling at the time."

---

[120] The Scullion - first introduced in "Sumerian Vortex: Music from a Lost Civilization", Amazon, 2020 - Chapter 17, p. 107

Publican: "Well, I was desperate - I had a duty not to deprive mankind of the collective wisdom of my social drinkers.

"After a lot of yoga and meditation, I decided to unsubstantiate the pub into a virtual venue for my social drinkers' problem-solving using Zoom to create a proto-Metaverse pub.

"To make our virtuality more real in a time of very onerous lockdowns, we elected to offer just-in-time trucked deliveries of fresh pints of porter, and food deliveries via bicycled messenger boys from our physical pub to the doorsteps of our isolated, home-bound social-drinkers."

Scullion: "I understand. There's nothing like fresh pints to stimulate the creative juices."

Publican: "This initial business strategy was so successful that we decided to acquire additional physical pubs, creating a network of pub-hubs for our delivery services and virtual problem solving. I approached a social fund VC for financing. She liked my business plan - by definition, it was very social."

Scullion: "At that point, how much capital did you take in, and what was the post-money valuation?"

VC: "By today's standards the capital raise was fairly modest at $160 million, and the valuation of the business was ridiculously high at $8 billion because there was a lot of competition for the deal."

Tbc...

Session 10.2

Recap of the Story (Part 2 of 5)

The Publican Gives a Press Interview

Headline: "How Much Is World Peace Worth?"

Dominic Geraghty

BYLINE: The Scullion[121], Managing Editor, "The Mayo Times"

Scullion, interviewing the Publican: "So, you raised a boatload of VC money for your pub-hub strategy. You were all rich - why bother solving any more world problems?"

Publican "Our richness was on paper only - we needed to create tangible value to crystallize our valuation...then we could engineer an exit event."

VC: "Geraghty's needed to move smartly to grow the business and create such an event - I wanted a cash return on my investment asap."

Publican: "And you kept the pressure on us!

"As Covid-19 restrictions decreased, Geraghty's pub-hubs reopened their physical spaces and suitably distanced social drinkers resumed their world problem-solving duties F2F. Their physical presences were complemented by Zoom collectives for those who couldn't attend in person."

Scullion: "How many social drinkers and Dead Viziers did you have at that point?"

Publican: "I remember the exact numbers - our network comprised 143 social drinkers at Geraghty's, three screens of 100 Zoomers each, and an infinite number of Dead Vizier advisors enjoying a vacation from the boredom of eternal bliss in heaven. We were growing rapidly - our business plan was forecasting 10,000 social drinkers in 2022, 100,000 in 2023, and 1,000,000 in 2025.

"On the basis of our new forecast and our performance to date, I raised a B Round of $500 million at $16 billion pre-money, and a later C Round of $750 million at a pre-money of $33 billion, thanks to my lead investor sitting here beside me."

VC: "It wasn't the least I could do!"

---

[121] The Scullion - first introduced in "Sumerian Vortex: Music from a Lost Civilization", Amazon, 2020 - Chapter 17, p. 107

Scullion: "That is very impressive."

Publican: "My social drinkers decided to prioritize the important problems of mankind they needed to solve. Our very wise Dead Viziers helped them. Six major contending problems to vote on were identified:

1. World Peace
2. Climate Change
3. Human of the Future
4. Personal Privacy
5. The Meaning of Life
6. The Deformation of Society.

"World Peace was the top vote-getter."

Scullion: "Well, it's an important problem to solve, but a lot of very astute people have been trying to create World Peace for the past 75 years to no avail. If anything, things are going in the opposite direction. How on earth could a small set of social drinkers, admittedly advised by the wisest dead people from all of history, come up with a solution?"

Head Pint: "The solution turned out to be quite simple. I should note here that we rely solely on supreme intuition during Geraghty's problem-solving sessions - analysis, research, note-taking (except on beer mats), and heaven-forbid, electronic devices are not permitted.

"The social drinkers, strongly influenced by the Dead Viziers, decided intuitively that the solution to World Peace was obvious: music. It just felt right. World-class scientists and Dead Vizier music composers strongly supported the solution concept."

Tbc...

Session 10.3

Recap of the Story (Part 3 of 5)

The Publican Gives a Press Interview

Headline: "Sound, Music, and the Survival of the Species"

BYLINE: The Scullion[122], Managing Editor of "The Mayo Times"

Scullion: "I bet that there were a lot of skeptics - how could mere music persuade the entire population of the world to embrace world peace?"

Head Pint: "It was not without some controversy - I had a lot of herding of cats to do along the way."

Scullion: "Ha-ha-ha! And how on earth - ahem - will you be able to design music that will appeal across cultures, never mind trigger the desired empathetic, loving emotions essential for World Peace?"

Publican: "That question is still under advisement at the moment - can I get back to you on that?"

Publican: "Now, to - it had to hang together biologically and scientifically - not just emotionally.

"So, they set themselves some questions to answer - what were the origins of music, how did it evolve, how does music create different emotions in our brains, what type of music, specifically, would be optimal for creating unifying, empathetic emotions across communities, and, lastly, how could we broadcast the completed World Peace music composition across the entire planet?"

Scullion: "Seems to me that those questions are practically intractable. I'm surprised that y'all did not give up right then and there!"

---

[122] The Scullion - first introduced in "Sumerian Vortex: Music from a Lost Civilization", Amazon, 2020 - Chapter 17, p. 107

Head Pint: "Well, almost everyone had personally experienced strong emotions at some point when listening to music. So, we knew that music could be transcendent - that it could create strong, spiritual, even euphoric emotions.

"If Geraghty's social drinkers could understand how these emotions were triggered by the brain's processing of music, perhaps they could design music that created a euphorium of universal empathy, thus enabling world peace.

"Our resident social-drinking neuroscientist helped us analyze how and why the brain processes music. Evidently, sound was critical for survival in pre-history - hearing and interpreting different sound frequencies was often a matter of life and death.

"Sounds were gradually structured into proto-music to catalyze social cohesion, thus increasing security, and it and rhythmic dancing also became part of reproduction rituals. Survival, socialization, and reproduction catalyzed a range of different emotions: fear, empathy, and love. These were associated with different kinds of structured sounds - that is, music.

"In effect, sound-as-music became the first proto-language. Our auditory cortex evolved into a highly sensitive instrument for recognizing different sound frequencies and combinations of sounds.

"So, our survival genes were hard-wired from the time of prehistoric humankind for sound and music interpretation and that wiring has endured through to the present time."

Scullion: "I hear you have special access to the head brain neuron - Chief Neuronimo - did that help you?"

Tbc...

Session 10.4

Recap of the Story (Part 4 of 5)

The Publican Gives a Press Interview

Headline: "Not Everyone is Thrilled by the Prospect of World Peace"

BYLINE: The Scullion [1], Managing Editor of "The Mayo Times"

Head Pint, responding: "Yes, definitely - Chief Neuronimo was of great help - he confirmed our theories about the importance of music for survival and confided that he is actually a drug-lord in charge of dispensing empathy drugs, among others, in the brain.

"However, we learned that he has problems - he's facing a revolution of his peon neurons. They have developed an addiction to serotonin and are complaining that they get disproportionately less than the music neurons.

"Plus, his executive neurons are very upset by this whole new transhuman thing - they do not feel that their natural, brain-processing capabilities need to be enhanced - they work just fine and who knows what untested, externally introduced enhancements would do to the brain's drug pipelines?"

Scullion: "Very concerning.

"However, you are making the case that music could conceivably release a flood of empathy brain-drugs that could create world peace under certain, as-yet hard-to-define circumstances. I suppose you have almost universal support for your very salutary quest?"

Publican: "Actually we have encountered surprisingly stiff opposition. Vested interests whose livelihoods depended on peacelessness - corporations, the military/industrial complex, governments, politicians, bureaucrats, policy experts, hegemonic nations, colonizers, the legal profession, and the U.N. expressed pious concerns about peacefulness.

"Of course, it's obvious that their objections stem from the fact that World Peace would interfere with their income, profits, or their position of power - they can't say that out loud, so they find other reasons to oppose our work.

"Global warming worriers have been particularly vociferous because they believe we should have voted for climate change as the most important problem to be solved - it is far more important than World Peace, they say."

Scullion: "But wouldn't World Peace accelerate global cooperation for solving climate change?"

Slow Pint jumped in: "You'd suppose so!

"Another problem we have is that our world is diverging, not converging - we are swimming against the tide - every day, we seem to move a little further away from peace. Societies are becoming more antagonistic, social media are being weaponized, and democracies are becoming more authoritarian. Whole nations are weaponizing their indigenous resources. The world is gradually de-globalizing as nations Balkanize in response [2].

"It isn't the most conducive time to achieve World Peace."

Dead Vizier Orwell, shaking his head sadly: "I was 40 years too late. I would like to retitle my book: '2024'."

Tbc...

[1] The Scullion - first introduced in "Sumerian Vortex: Music from a Lost Civilization", Amazon, 2020 - Chapter 17, p. 107
[2] "1984 + 38 + ?: A Scenario for a New World Order", 2022, Amazon

Comments:

JI: Timely sentiments given the peaceless swing in global politics and growing conservative (authoritarian!) governments. Even music has become more conservative, thus thwarting a peaceful path to peace. The choice of the masses who still vote suggest peace may come about via a global authoritarian cabal that relabels war as cultural rehabilitation through thinning the populace of critical thinkers who also speak up... and thought police will not be far behind. That pendulum swing takes patience and a few generations for each cycle. I think I'm ready for a long winter nap.

Session 10.5

Recap of the Story (Part 5 of 5)

The Publican Gives a Press Interview

Headline: "It Looks Like We'll Need a Plan B"

BYLINE: The Scullion[123], Managing Editor of "The Mayo Times"

Slow Pint: "Look, the Ukraine invasion happened just as Covid was easing. These two events caused enormous trickle-down - maybe gush-down is a better word - effects globally that are negatively affecting the prospects for World Peace.

"Lately, we at Geraghty's are spending more time discussing societal divisiveness and geopolitics rather than the creation of music for World Peace. We can't ignore these societal changes since they affect our potential music solution so profoundly."

Scullion: "Still, it seems that you have made a lot of progress and developed a world-wide following of social drinkers. So, given your success to date, why would you be interested in an alliance with Mayo Nation?"

Publican: "We've heard about an ancient music system in Mayo that creates euphoria and collective empathy across its population during your annual Harmony Day. If we could combine its capabilities with our

---

[123] The Scullion - first introduced in "Sumerian Vortex: Music from a Lost Civilization", Amazon, 2020 - Chapter 17, p. 107

World Peace music composition, we might still have a chance to reach our global goal."

Scullion: "So, I'm sensing that Mayo could be part of your Plan B."

Publican: "Possibly! We are open to an alliance, but we need to get to know the Mayo Nation and Mayoans better - hence this visit. Plus, we would like to experience your Harmony Day.

"In view of the non-conducive-to-peace world events, we have been considering downsizing our World Peace goal to a Regional Peace goal. Assuming the feeling is mutual, we could start with a small-sized nation like Mayo and prove our thesis on a limited scale. If successful, we'd be creating a foundation stone from which to expand peace regionally at first and then globally eventually.

"From what we've heard so far, Mayo's philosophy of living fits well with ours. Plus, Mayo has made great strides implementing its Grand Plan[2] and its Guided Communitarian Democracy[124] with an associated constitution we appreciate and respect. We can offer a valuable, worldwide network and most importantly, the unique wisdom of our social drinkers and the Dead Viziers.

"So, that's why we are here in Mayo..."

Scullion: "Well, an alliance is an intriguing concept, and I very much hope that it comes to fruition. Good luck with your visit. Our readers will wait with bated breath for the results of your due diligence."

Publican: "Thank you, William."

---

[124] See: "Sumerian Vortex - Mayo Goes Mental", Amazon, 2021

Dominic Geraghty

Topic #11:

Precap of Music for World Peace Saga

Session 11.1

Precap of Upcoming Events and a New Character Appears in the Music-for-World-Peace Saga

By now, you'll have twigged that my saga is allegorical - that is, it doesn't mean what it says, and it means what it doesn't say. And yes, my music-for-World-Peace saga is hard to follow - it stutters incrementally in 3,000-character-maximum posts and sometimes whimsically deviates from the straight and narrow of the main theme...but...

The saga meanders because I'm emulating what you'd normally experience when socially drinking in the familiar surroundings of your local pub. Pub conversations don't move in a straight line. There are interruptions, surprises, disappointments, deviations, pontifications, annoyances, crazy ideas, trite clichés, insights, gratuitous quotes, and below-the-surface seriousness. However, one thing I can guarantee in Geraghty's: Atlas shall not shrug.

Considering the inevitable detours, you deserve to know the story line (assuming there is one). So, here's a precap of what the future holds for our friends, the social drinkers:

Geraghty's team - the Publican, Head Pint, Slow Pint, Flaming Cosmo, Double Red Bull, plus various Dead Viziers - visits Mayo Nation in the west of Ireland to experience Harmony Day.

The music of Harmony Day creates population-wide euphoria during their visit - all are amazed at the feeling of peace that ensues when their out-of-body consciousnesses merge together at the climax of the music for a timeless period into what Mayoans call "The One".

Wait! I'm feeling a mysterious, imperious presence.

The No-One: "Greetings humans! I've news for y'all: sorry to disappoint, but humankind is merely an experiment of the Gods – yes, that's me and mine, the one and the all - I'm singular and I'm plural - we'll use the royal 'we' to simplify things, shall we?

"Dear Plotinus of Rome wasn't too far off base with his concept of 'The One' - the first principle of all - the cause of being for everything else in the universe - but he didn't know about the 'NO' part of our name. And, back in the day, how was he to know that we were a complex number? That is, when we're here, we're not here, and when we're not here, we're here. We'll get to that later…"

"We've been watching your human machinations with glee for centi-mega-years! You're very entertaining – the randomness of your free will lends a delightful unpredictability to it all - even though there's no such thing as free will, you know."

Chief Neuronimo: "Hmmm… I've a bone to pick with Your Regal Godliness. During Harmony Day, my consciousness went AWOL in an out-of-body-experience, but you won't tell me how this happened: 'There are some things only a God should know', you said. Meanwhile, my peon-neurons saw my authority being blatantly undermined - they knew that I'd never give my consciousness permission to leave the cranium."

The No-One: "So sorry, mate, I'm sure. Being human and having a consciousness are one and the same thing - but sometimes the consciousness goes walkabout. However, NO harm done – didn't your consciousness return of its own volition?"

Tbc…

Comments:

JI: Dom, thanks for the over-the-Cliff Notes for your stories. I've fallen and don't want to get up from your phantasmagorical dreams. Carry on, mate.

DG: Jeff, you give me hope!!! I will try to keep you on a high. I'm a daydream believer…D.

P.S. Very enjoyable wording!

HG: This is all getting even deeper and deeper. Love the oxymorons and the focus on consciousness. Reminds me of you-know-who.

DG: Well, a pint is very deep water - I hope that we shall plumb the depths together. Thank you - pleased to be recognized as contradictory and a fan of consciousness. Je suivrai le prêtre Jésuite jusqu'au point Oméga avec toi!!!

Session 11.2

Precap of Upcoming Events and a Detour into Strategies for Coping with the Disappointment of Mortality

The No-One: "Look, I came here to talk about me, not youse, capisce?

"I've never experienced what it's like to be a human. I've heard about time-zones on earth, but I live in eternity, that is, timelessness – no clocks needed. I tele-transport at the speed of light in NO time at all. I've NO jetlag since I'm not Circadian.

"I don't need a body to exist – I just am and always have been. I can't imagine what it must feel like to be a human experiencing non-everlasting, limited time, after which oblivion is expected. Imagine - there's NO continuity: 'Boom! – sorry, my friend, your life's now over, goodbye forever!'

"Except, of course, there's a thin strand of continuity through the imperceptible evolution of passed-on genes – that was the oh-so-clever tweak I added early on to my multi-mega-year human experiment."

Buddhist in Geraghty's Stupa-Bar in Yangon, sipping strong Rangoon tea: "Aren't you forgetting something, Your NO-Oneness? The reincarnation cycle guarantees me continuity until I reach nirvana, which I hear might take a while."

The No-One: "Even if my human experiment could accommodate reincarnation - and I'm not saying it does - it's a risky bet. You mightn't come back as a human - you could end up being a butterfly with a lifetime of just one day - how many cycles would you like?"

"Death - what a waste of all that hard-won experience in time-limited humans' lives! How do y'all deal with the impending, unavoidable disappointment of death: that your life's a meaningless grain in the eternal sands of time?"

Schopenhauer: "There - I was right all along - life is pointless - it's better not to have been born, and if born, it's better to die as quickly as possible!"

Silenus: "My dear Artie, I couldn't agree more! Man's a suffering creature...the very best thing for man is totally unreachable: not to have been born, not to exist, to be nothing. The second-best thing...is to die soon."

Slow Pint: "You both must have had very jolly funerals...

"Deal with it we do, your Godliness! Humans take two approaches for coping with their looming deaths:

"Some do the best they can for the time they have on earth, knowing that they cannot go all the way to solving the meaning of life, but they can contribute some progress - they hope that their labor will be carried on after they die and enter oblivion – that's a form of continuity that offsets the devastating disappointment of their mortality.

"Other humans believe that there's an entity which was, is - and will be - the primary cause of everything. This entity was the 'first' and nothing was before. Plotinus called this entity 'The One' - he believed it was equivalent to Plato's 'the Good'. For these believers, dying is a threshold to another life where the divine human soul previously living in exile on earth fulfils its desire to return 'home' to 'The One'. Descartes would be pleased.

"Plus...let me emphasize that there is no 'No' in 'The One'!"

Tbc...

Comments:

JI: Hurry back, Dom. We're all hanging by a thread to the pointlessness of waiting for your next installment. But wait, we will.

DG: Thanks. It is a distinct honor to be pointless. I've achieved my life goal sooner than I expected and I didn't even have to die to get there. There is much more pointlessness in store.

HG: A lot of pints to swallow here. I'm way past my usual limits, but still thirsty!

DG: Some of my points are hard to swallow - a sad day would be a pintless one. I will continue to make a point to slake your thirst, but I cannot promise not to be pointless. Keep up the good work!

Acknowledgments

A heartfelt thank you to the many commenters who over the past 2 years humorously word-jousted with me on LinkedIn and suggested creative new ideas for me to pursue. I have included some of your comments and suggestions in this book using your initials only.

About the Author

Dominic Geraghty has a B.E. and a Ph.D. in Chemical Engineering and an MBA. After working in the Irish government to deploy advanced energy technologies, he emigrated to the U.S. in the late 1970s. With an extensive career as a venture capitalist and CEO, president, and executive chairman of various high-tech companies in North America, Dom is well-versed in business and technology. This experience and his passions for music, ancient civilizations, small nation development, and travel appear with Irish humor in the lines of his first and second novels of the Sumerian Vortex saga, his more serious, humor-tinged book '1984 + 38 + ?- A Scenario for a New World Order', "The Pub People – Volume 1: Laughter Is the Music of Peace", and his biweekly columns on LinkedIn recounting the antics of Geraghty' Pub's social drinkers, selections from which form the content of this book.

Married to Eva, an Austrian, Dom splits time between homes in Northern California, the Leeward Islands, and southern Bavaria.

Coming Next:

"The Pub People"
Volume 3

Previously Published by Dominic Geraghty:

"Sumerian Vortex - Music from a Lost Civilization", 2020

"Sumerian Vortex - Mayo Goes Mental", 2021

"1984 + 38 + ? - A Scenario for a New World Order", 2022

"The Pub People – Volume 1: Laughter Is the Music of Peace", 2022

For more information, please email
dominic@sumerianvortex.com, or visit our website:
www.sumerianvortex.com